Sweets and Toxins

Christopher Woodall

SWEETS AND TOXINS

Stories

DALKEY ARCHIVE PRESS

Library of Congress Cataloging-in-Publication Data
Names: Woodall, Christopher, 1953- author.
Title: Sweets and toxins : stories / Christopher Woodall.
Description: First Dalkey Archive edition. | McLean, IL : Dalkey
      Archive Press, 2018.
Identifiers: LCCN 2018026159|ISBN 9781628972924 (pbk.:alk.
      paper)
Classification: LCC PR6123.O5278 A6 2018 | DDC 823/.92--dc23
LC record available at https://lccn.loc.gov/2018026159

www.dalkeyarchive.com
McLean, IL / Dublin

Contents

Sweets and Toxins

Loved to Pieces

FIRST SHE FELT broken, simply broken. Then, in succession: numb, angry, in fear for her sanity, calm, anaesthetized, empty as a conch. Briefly she was determined to get even with him somehow, anyhow; until one day she discovered that hatred had no lasting purchase on her, revenge exerted no enduring appeal. Nauseous with self-contempt, she began to dismiss the entire course of her private life, accusing herself of weakness. All this suffering! And for what! For a man who had only seemed to love her and who now, evidently, no longer did. Pitiful. Ridiculous. The banality of it!

In the first days and weeks after John had made his shame-faced confession, packed his bags and gone, only Julie's work could distract her. Each morning, as she closed her car door and strode into school, she would dry her eyes and confect a smile; ten or eleven hours later, as she settled back behind the steering wheel, she would well up again and drive home through the resulting blur. In her flat, she kept one radio in the kitchen-diner, the other in her bedroom, both tuned to talk.

What John had done to her felt like a rape but, weirdly, creepily, a rape perpetrated in reverse. He had long been inside her – just where, indeed, she had been happy to have him – occupying her mind, body, soul, moulding from within all her habits and senses, her very impulses and thoughts. Just when she had grown to feel reliant on the depleted oxygen from his lungs merely to breathe, and on the second-hand words that tumbled so easily from his mouth merely to think, he had withdrawn abruptly, without eliciting consent, without seeking permission, ripping himself from her, leaving her floored and broken, simply broken. Never had she been so vulnerable, never had she been so hurt.

Julie's recovery was slow for, although departed, John remained somehow ubiquitous, a live presence that receded only by degrees, as if tiptoeing backwards, a figure apt to flicker at any moment across a shaft of light, or to be sighted squatting in a patch of early evening gloom. Diaphanous traces of the man, like insubstantial fossils, kept appearing, as if to torment her. His spices had gone from her kitchen shelves, but his cooking continued to shape her cravings, lingering as a fund of memories in her taste buds. Shared bedding had been discarded, carpets cleaned, his few remaining clothes thrown out, yet the fragrance of the man continued sporadically to invade her nostrils. She had stacked his old CDs and vinyl in her garage for eventual collection, but still his favourite music rose unbidden to her throat or insinuated itself between her lips.

Arriving home one evening after a happily mind-dulling day at school, Julie dashed to the floor the wineglass from which she had just taken a first sip: she had caught herself lifting it to her lips with a flourish idiosyncratic, if not unique, to John. At school the following day, while speaking at a staff meeting, a wave of revulsion had surged through her as she caught John inside her mouth, heavy on her tongue, sprawling across one of his own pet words, which *she* had just voiced in his hitherto inimitable sneer. John was everywhere: in the books upon her shelves; in the colour coordination of the plants in her garden; in the custard-yellow scouring pads he'd purchased in bulk and which she still spotted each time she opened *that* cupboard door; in the vacancy on what remained 'his side' of the bed; in the loneliness of her dreamless sleep.

Almost a year had passed when, one early summer evening, at the end of a satisfying week of teaching, Julie was standing at her chopping board, her radios all silent now, humming a song from her steadily evolving personal playlist. She was preparing the rich beef daube she had promised herself for weeks but to which, until very recently, she had felt unentitled: as if a beef daube might properly be devoured only by a person of robust constitution and happy outlook. Sensing a movement outside her window, she glanced up to see John getting out of his car, walking the short gravel path to her door, his chest out but his head lowered, looking, as ever, simultaneously cowed and proud. Abandoned in the passenger seat, a young woman – his new lover, presumably – could be viewed in frozen profile: her hair long and brown, her forehead slight, her nose rather pointed.

Julie finished dicing the stewing steak, then walked to her front door and opened it, cleaver in hand. With an exuberantly false smile, John said hello. Then, noticing the cleaver, he started back. Julie looked down at the smeared blade and laughed shortly. 'I wouldn't demean myself,' she said.

John mumbled that he'd intended to come for his music sooner. Julie pointed the cleaver at the garage door, accessible from the flat's tiny hallway: 'Help yourself.'

At the chopping board, Julie's breath came fast, in spite of herself. She lay the cleaver down and picked up a paring knife, discovering she had to lean against the kitchen counter to steady herself. I'm all right, she said beneath her breath. She began to peel her vegetables: a swede, two turnips, one potato. For months, she had willed John to return, rehearsing the posture she might strike and the words she might speak, sometimes pleading on bended knee, sometimes lunging at him wildly. And now?

John was right there at her flat, back inside her vital space, shuttling between her garage and his car. At least his woman had stayed put, decorously staring at her knees. Or perhaps reading? Or contemplating eternity?

One peeled turnip later, John stood at Julie's kitchen door, clearing his throat and surveying her. She looked up but could find nothing whatever to say. Meanwhile, a smile appeared on his face. Perhaps he imagined he had understood something. 'How have you been?' he asked. 'Get lost, John,' Julie replied. He nodded. Only then did Julie register the question he had asked. 'Never better,' she shouted to his departing back. John broke his stride but didn't turn round.

Standing away from her window, Julie watched the car pull out from the kerb. She went to look in the garage. John's last things had gone, leaving a precise John's-things-sized gap, a final careless insult. In a frenzy, Julie threw neighbouring boxes and bags and oddments from left and right into the gap until it was less than a memory.

That night, having done scant justice to the daube, Julie went to bed and wept for the first time in months. Yet she felt relieved that John's last possessions had gone and that there was no reason to see him again. She was glad also to have glimpsed his new woman. Her tears came more slowly than before and no longer burned her cheeks, feeling lukewarm to her now. She was quite unable to sob. This was the last time she would ever cry over John. She stretched out across the entire breadth and length of her bed, luxuriating in the space that she had by this point fully reclaimed. She sank into a peaceful, restorative sleep. Towards daybreak, a dream came to her.

She dreamt she was standing in the middle of her kitchen-diner when the doorbell rang. Outside, at the kerb, the postman's van was parked. On opening the door, she saw there was nobody there. At her feet, extending from her red-brick doorstep down onto the path, lay an irregularly shaped brown parcel, well over a metre and a half in length, one corner of which was stained an uneven purple. Looking up, she saw the post van moving off, an unfamiliar woman at the wheel, long brown hair topped by a peaked cap.

It took all Julie's strength to drag the parcel into her flat and then, having cleared the kitchen table, to hoist the parcel onto it. Standing back, she noticed that the purplish stain at the corner of the parcel had spread. She touched it with a tentative, probing finger, which came away sticky and red. 'Nobody sends me meat through the post,' she whispered in her dream, raising finger to nose.

With kitchen scissors materialising in her right hand, Julie cut away at the paper and cardboard. Meat, indeed! A first peek beneath the wrapping revealed a jumble of body parts. She noticed her former lover's left foot, with its flapping fleshy mole at the ankle – the only part of his body ever to have repelled her. She recognized his left hip, its rust-coloured oval birthmark. Since John's innards had been discarded, there was no stink to offend the nostrils, merely the sweet pong of blood and freshly deceased human flesh. Jointed like a hare, everything essential was present: the two arms, upper and lower; the neck; the two legs, upper and lower; the handsome head; the trunk including the evacuated abdomen, tidily resealed and sutured; the forlorn penis with its shrivelled pendant sack; the feet and the hands.

Pleased to have John returned to her safekeeping, and comforted that nothing essential was missing, Julie, ever a stickler for presentation, was disturbed by the disorder, the bloody jumble, the gaudy mess of it all. She had to put things right.

In kitchen gloves now, Julie recomposed the puzzle of John's body, placing each part gently but firmly in correct relation to each other, right hand meeting right forearm, head adjoining neck, and so on. Having completed the tableau, she attended to John's face, pinching some colour into his cheeks and tugging his lips into the semblance of a smile. Then, each of her hands gripping the edge of her kitchen table, she bowed low over the cadaver and laid her head sideways in her former lover's spotless lap, embracing his remains.

'I'm so pleased to have you back with me,' she murmured in her dream, wishing John could hear her. 'You are no longer quite the man you were, but I wouldn't have you any other way now.'

The bell rang again but this time the ringing continued. Julie dreamt that she rose from the table and went to the door but once again there was no one there and still the bell kept ringing. She stared at the word PRESS printed in black gothic letters across the white bell button. She covered her ears and shook her head, waking now, swinging an arm out to hit the alarm.

Seated on the edge of her bed, her feet squarely in the heart of her sheepskin rug, Julie pondered each detail of her dream, eager to impress it upon her waking mind, clinging to every precious detail.

Then she rose and threw back the curtain. It had rained and the sun shone through the trees and down onto the shrubs in her small back garden. There was a light breeze.

Surprising herself, Julie burst into song, belting out an old swing tune, a favourite of John's, but making it her own now, indelibly her own. And, with that song ringing from her throat and lips, she went through to the kitchen to clear up the previous evening's mess.

'All of me,' she sang, 'Why not take all of me? Can't you see? I'm no good without you . . .'

Dave, Danielle, and Tom

EVEN AFTER TOM and Danielle set up house together, I'd stay at his – or, rather, at *their* – place, whenever I was in the country, which was quite often. Later, we'd meet at a pub but I would have to go and sleep at some other friend's place – which was awkward. Later still, when I phoned to say I was in town, Tom would make excuses not to see me. Once he told me that a mid-morning phone call was insufficient notice: he had a wife and kids, right? By the time I'd returned to live in this country and had moved into a flat across the river, we'd lost touch. All on account of a canary. Though Danielle probably wouldn't see it that way.

Dave was a total pain in the neck. I was so delighted when Tom lost interest in seeing him. I never liked the guy, never understood what Tom saw in him. Apparently, they were close at university and afterwards shared a squat in Peckham: their glory days! They were changing the world one lousy song, one scrappy demo, one smudgy leaflet at a time. On the only occasion I went to the pub with them they got so drunk and talked so much and forgot so completely that I was there that I think I got to hear their entire salad-days shtick. It was like Silence and Shallow – but in their thirties, for Christ's sake. Oh the days that we have seen! Embarrassing. Good riddance.

I was fond of Dave. He made me laugh. He was still leading the kind of carefree life we'd both enjoyed when we were young.

He hadn't stopped getting into trouble with women, was still barely scraping a living, and kept throwing time and commitment at political lost causes. He even played the guitar still and went busking. To cap it all, he was living in Europe. I'd always dreamed of living in Europe but had never had Dave's flair for languages or his ability to rub along with people. So, for a while at least, it was great to meet up. He made me laugh and he made me nostalgic. More importantly, he made me feel comfortable about my own, much safer, life choices.

For several years things were fine between me and Danielle. The evening Tom introduced us, we went for a drink and told her all about our university exploits. She laughed her head off, kept buying rounds, eager to hear more. From that point on, she and I would tease each other whenever we met. She'd poke fun at my lifestyle, ask me what nationality of woman I was seeing this week – that kind of thing. I'd laugh at her pretensions, her careerism, her craving for the latest consumer gadget or fashion accessory. If we never exactly hit it off, we certainly had a modus vivendi. I was Tom's best friend; she was his partner, subsequently his wife: I figured we just had to get along.

The first few times Dave stayed over, everything went more or less okay. Tom would cook a nice meal which we'd wash down with whatever bottle of cheapskate wine Dave had purchased from the corner shop on his stroll from the tube. After supper, Tom and I would put the kids to bed while Dave would do the dishes – though, of course, we always had to do them all again the following day: Dave had never heard of rinsing. Then Tom would put on his naughty-schoolboy face and ask whether I minded if they went down the pub. I'd grit my teeth and say, Of course not, have fun, *lads!* Then I'd settle with a book or, most likely, catch up with a bit of work.

It was probably my fault things went wrong. I should have seen it coming. Dave's arrival in town always felt like an excuse to let my hair down, drink more than usual, fool myself I was still a free agent. Maybe Dani didn't approve but she wouldn't interfere. I imagined she was fine with our friendship. So as soon as we got out of the house – provided the weather was okay – we'd get some cans and walk for miles, talking and fooling, or stopping at different pubs. Dave was a great raconteur and his anecdotes about life abroad and the jobs he took on and the corners he painted himself into were great entertainment. And we'd always bump into people Dave hadn't seen for years.

Though it didn't bother me, I found Tom and Danielle's home pretty strange: it was so ordered and pristine I was terrified of putting a mug down on a sideboard without first locating a coaster. At university, I'd been the tidy, punctilious, ordered one; yet now Tom was living in something between an ideal home and an ICU – you could hardly imagine a more sterile environment. Except they had kids of course. Danielle's hair and clothes and general demeanour became steelier, more businesslike, crisper, and colder each time we met. As for those children, by the time they started school they could freeze me at twenty paces with the remote precision of their social etiquette. It wasn't natural. And then the canaries. Those fucking canaries.

One of the very first things that brought Tom and me together was our love of pet birds. On only our second date we spotted a canary in a park, recognized its distress, caught it, then traced its owners. It was both an adventure and a blessing on our nascent love. Several years passed before we did anything more about this common interest, but eventually we went out and bought three near-identical canaries: since we weren't yet married it felt like a trial consecration. When we got the birds home we opened a bottle of Champers and held a little ceremony and named them Bish, Bash, and Bosh, though Tom could never quite tell them apart: he was forever getting Bosh and Bish mixed up.

The parting of the ways, the big bust-up, didn't come completely out of the blue. Danielle had been really stressed. Somebody at work had been unjustly promoted over her. Coincidentally, the following week I'd had a chance for promotion but had turned it down: a colleague in my department had mentioned I was a shoo-in for deputy-head. My reaction was: So what? Dani was livid, called me a flake, said I lacked ambition. 'I'm a teacher,' I told her, 'I love to teach, I love being in the classroom, that's what I do, that's all I want to do, and, god knows, it already entails quite enough pointless form-filling these days.' Dani apologized. But I should never have told her. She hadn't needed to know.

As usual, we'd come in late and pissed – especially Tom, who'd been bawled out by Danielle earlier that day for some misstep he was too loyal to divulge, and had accordingly hit the whisky – always a bad idea. We'd managed the stairs and reached the landing okay but then Tom, bless him, tripped on a toy train and crashed into a clothes horse, and the lights all went up. We'd woken one of the sprogs – a hanging offence, apparently. Next morning, breakfast was worse than a wake. Not a word spoken. So when the kids went upstairs to brush their 'toothy-pegs,' I attempted to lighten the atmosphere. Earlier, in the living room, I'd noticed one of the canaries was missing. My solicitous enquiry was not appreciated.

The last straw was not that Tom and Dave had come in plastered and reeking of smoke, nor that they'd woken me and the kids and trampled mud up the stairs: I could put up with that once a year, even twice. Boys will be boys. Even when they're grown men. I get that. No, the last straw was the following morning and Dave's flippant attitude to our loss, our bereavement. And the tolerant, amused attitude Tom adopted towards Dave's flip-pancy. When Dave came downstairs he must have popped his head round the living room door and noticed Bish was missing. I don't know which was more stupid of me: to expect loyalty and support from my hungover husband or heartfelt condolences from his loutish friend . . .

With hindsight, I can see that with Bish gone it was an accident – a collision – just waiting to happen. Dani was soppy about those canaries and Dave never liked them, never cared for pets in general and was not the most empathetic person and certainly hadn't a diplomatic bone in his body. Despite the fact I'd had a good soak, taken painkillers and downed orange juice and black coffee in roughly equal proportions, I still felt like death. We were both in the doghouse. Nobody was talking. Then Dave said he'd noticed a canary was missing. He remembered their names. 'Which is it? Bish, Bosh, or Bash? Don't tell me one of them fell off their perch.' He was grinning infectiously. I couldn't help myself.

I probably did phrase the question somewhat facetiously. It got a laugh out of Tom though, which wasn't bad considering the hangover he was nursing. Danielle gave him a cold, hard stare. 'Bish died,' she announced, centering her cup carefully in its saucer. I'd never seen anyone look so solemn. It was hard not to laugh. 'My condolences!' I said, raising my teacup to hide my grin. 'How did it go?' I asked. 'How did what go?' 'Bish,' I said. '*She*,' Danielle said. 'Sorry. How did *she* go? A bad cold? The measles? What do canaries die of, anyway?' '*You* tell him what happened,' Danielle said to Tom. It was like a challenge. Poor Tom. Could he possibly pull it off with a straight face?

I was grieving, okay? Is a canary too small, too insignificant to grieve over? Any pet you love – even a gerbil or a spider – can evoke grief by dying. It's about us, it's not about them. If we love, we grieve: period. So, Bish's death was still quite recent and I was hurting. I couldn't talk about it. Not to someone who doesn't care a fig for either pets or for pet-owners' feelings. That's why I asked Tom to answer Dave's questions. 'Danielle,' he began, 'arrived home from work one day to find Bish flat on her back, claws in the air.' When I saw Tom's ear-to-ear smile, I got up and left the kitchen. As I closed the door, the room exploded with laughter.

It was deeply insensitive of me. It isn't funny that Bash and Bosh pecked Bish to death. And it was one thing for Dave to joke about a remake of Hitchcock's *The Birds* with canaries in the title roles, but I should have kept a straight face and shown Danielle more respect – and Bish too, for that matter. However, with my finer feelings still dulled by alcohol, Dave's sense of the ridiculous carried all before it. When I told him, as straightforwardly as I could, that we'd called the vet and the vet had explained that because the birds were siblings – triplets, as it were – they had never established a proper pecking order, Dave burst into peals of laughter and, well, I'm afraid I joined in.

While we were – how to put it? – screeching with laughter, Danielle stormed back into the room. I don't think I've ever seen anyone so angry. She was stamping from one foot to the other like a parrot on speed. This wasn't funny. Tom wiped away his tears and smiled up at her, shrugging like a bashful, wayward child. Danielle wagged her finger, literally calling him out: 'When you've quite finished, might I have a word with you alone in the living room?' 'Trouble!' I tremoloed. But what could I do? I just cut myself one last slice of toast with lashings of Danielle's home-made three-citrus marmalade, telling myself I'd finally solved the mystery of how Tom could feel at ease in a roomful of boisterous schoolchildren.

Angry? I was more hurt than angry. Tom just didn't seem to understand. He kept begging me to calm down. As if *I* were being unreasonable. I reminded him how much he too had loved Bish. 'They were our babies,' I told him. 'No,' he replied, 'our babies were our babies.' 'But we had Bish, Bosh, and Bash first,' I said. Then, pausing for effect, I said, 'I don't want Dave staying here again.' 'What? Because he doesn't care about a dead canary?' 'No. Because he doesn't care that we care about a dead canary. He's heartless, cold. I don't want him around.' 'Dave's my oldest friend,' Tom mumbled. 'But this is *our* home,' I said. 'If you're not going to tell him, I will.'

While Dani was upstairs, I had a quiet word with Dave. He was trying to make light of it all: 'Sorry I got you into trouble with the missus,' he said. Referring to Dani as 'the missus' really annoyed me. He was trying to get me to laugh at her – or *about* her. I wasn't having that. 'You need to understand one thing, Dave. The time of my life wasn't at university or in that squat, getting pissed and pulling women. The time of my life is here and now, with Danielle upstairs making herself presentable for the office and the kids stuffing their satchels for school. And, yeah, the canaries cooing in their cage.' Dave looked aghast. 'Jesus, Tom. Whatever happened?' 'I grew up.'

Things were different after that. I'd phone whenever I was in town and occasionally we'd meet up, but mostly we wouldn't. Either Tom was tired or Danielle was working late and there was no one to look after the kids. Once, when we hadn't met up for over a year, he came straight out and said, 'I just fancy a quiet evening in.' The last time I phoned him, I said, 'I'm assuming you're going to put me off. Just tell me why. Is it Danielle?' Tom laughed, sounding shockingly happy and carefree. 'I'm simply not in the mood to drink and talk about old times. Because that's all we do. That's all we have.' I was sad he'd said that. I still miss him.

I got my way. Dave hasn't been back and Tom hasn't seen him for a while – which of course is up to him. Bish and Bash died a couple of years ago and we now have a cat. I was thinking this over as we got into bed the other evening and I couldn't help laughing. 'What is it?' Tom asked. 'I was thinking how a life or a relationship can turn on an event that at the time seems insignificant.' 'Like?' 'Well, don't laugh . . . but I suddenly felt grateful to Bish and the brutal way she died. If it took the death of a canary to mature my husband . . .' I completed the shocking thought in silence: After all, what's one canary more or less?

Sitting in your armchair, you may not like this ending. You might prefer me to rebel, kick over the traces, reclaim whatever youthful fire I once possessed. You might – like Dave – think Danielle is to blame. But Dani's good to me. And I have other

Lying to Be Cruel

I WITNESSED A psychodrama yesterday. I think that's what it was. In fact, I played a part in it.

I was in Copenhagen to run my monthly seminar on social dynamics. The university gives me a room for the night and a canteen dinner, both adequate.

For once, however, on retreating to my room, I felt I needed company or at least conversation. I glanced at the screen in the corner then, knowing my wife would be too busy to talk to me, phoned my son in Hamburg but he was busy too. On an impulse, I decided to look up Jeanette, a woman I had a relationship with many, many years ago. If she were alive – and why wouldn't she be? – it wouldn't take long to track her down: she was the kind of person you could never imagine existing anywhere outside Copenhagen.

After some expressions of surprise and other preliminaries, when I said I happened to be in the city for the night she said I should come and have dinner.

You'll meet Per, she said.

Per? I said. *That* Per?

Sure, she replied, with a little laugh. Then she said where they lived and told me they ate at seven thirty.

*

Per turned out to be a shambling, bohemian type, an amateur jazz musician, and either much older than me and Jeanette, or markedly less well preserved. Jeanette seemed the same as before: nervy, bright, angular, but reserved too. I was reminded why I'd fallen for her and how upset I'd been when she'd jilted me. I recalled her frank explanation: 'You're fun and I do love you. But Per needs me. You don't.'

She had been right, I suppose, but it had taken me several years to get over it, perhaps because her 'I do love you' kept ringing in my ears, an engine of equally unfounded hope and regret. The first New Year after we separated, I received a card. Per had moved in with her and they were 'trying for a baby.' I hadn't wanted to know that and I never replied. After a few years when I fell in love again, I hurried into a marriage that has always been good enough but rarely joyful.

I was now sitting in their dining room, hearing Per's anecdotes, while Jeanette bustled about the kitchen, preparing a tagine. Against one wall, under some historic concert posters, stood an upright piano flanked by matching rickety music stands, each carrying ill secured sheet music; a trumpet lay in a dilapidated leather armchair. The wall shelving was stacked not only with books but with every sort of knickknack, card, and photo of grinning or pouting children, none of whom, Per divulged, were theirs. Mostly nephews and nieces, he said.

Ordinarily, when people ask me if I have children, I'm unembarrassed, matter-of-fact. On this occasion, I dreaded the question and when it came – with all the leaden inevitability of conversational etiquette – I was momentarily tempted to 'delete' one or two of them. Four, I said, finally. Then, as if in mitigation: Though two of them are twins.

Jeanette brought in the tagine and side dishes, placing them all on the oval mat that occupied the centre of the table. Per uncorked the wine I had brought; Jeanette served.

Did you know Wolf has four kids? Per asked.

Jeanette's eyes squeezed half-shut for an instant. Four? That must be nice, she said.

During the meal, we talked of anything but children: Per's performances, compositions, and teaching; Jeanette's work for the city council and her political commitments; my books and conferences and consultancy. Repeatedly, I heard myself sounding either complacent about my achievements or apologetic. There were several moments when none of us spoke at all.

I was still picking at a damson and cinnamon tart that Jeanette had 'thrown together' for the occasion when Per pushed back his chair and said: It's great to meet you at last, Wolf. I've heard about you over the years. If Jeanette and I seem a little muted, well . . . (here he turned to his wife) . . . shall I tell him about Tina?

Why ever not? Jeanette said, getting up to open a window and fetching a box of Toscanellos from the kitchen. Per lit his with a lighter and held out the flame for his wife.

We've had a bit of a shock, Per said, resuming his seat. Jeanette nodded in corroboration.

I'll tell it my way, Per said, looking at his wife. You can always interrupt, darling, if I misremember some detail.

Sure, Jeanette said, funnelling smoke from both nostrils.

A couple of weeks ago, he began, we were seated here at this table, just the two of us, after lunch. It was a Sunday. Jeanette was sitting where you are now, flicking through a newspaper. I was about to do the dishes. Sunday domesticity, you know? Per appeared to ponder this for a moment.

The phone rang and you got up to answer it, Jeanette prompted.

That's right. We get a lot of nuisance calls, even Sundays, even sometimes – as on this occasion – in English. So when I heard a voice say, 'Hi, I'm Tina,' I gave my standard nuisance-call response: 'I don't know who you are or what you want but please cross me off your list and do have a nice day,' and put the phone down. But she phoned straight back. Before I could get a word out, she said, 'Listen. I'm your daughter and my mother always told me you were at least a polite person and you're not being polite.' 'My daughter?' I said. 'Like hell, you are. I don't have a daughter.' At this point, I noticed Jeanie had pushed her paper aside and was removing her glasses.

Per paused and Jeanette took up the story.

The next thing I heard Per say was: 'You're British, aren't you? English, I'd guess. Yorkshire?'

That's exactly what I said, Per confirmed. And Tina replied: 'Uh-huh. South Yorkshire. Like my mother. Which is why you recognize the accent. Remember now? Sheffield? 1993?'

I didn't hear that part, Jeanette said. But I could see Per was drawing up a chair – the chair you're sitting on right now, in point of fact. Then he said, staring at me, his eyes wide open, 'So – *Tina*, did you say? – you think you're my daughter?' At this point I got up and went and stood beside him and he put the phone on speaker.

'Look,' Tina was saying, 'If you don't believe me, give me some DNA and I'll prove it. My mother did sleep around a bit in those days. You were by no means the only one. But she's sure it was you. The condom split . . .'

Per coughed, as if the cigar or the memory – or, perhaps, the persistent lack of memory – disagreed with him. Then he took back the story from his wife.

'So how old are you?' I asked Tina.

'All grown up. Work it out,' she replied.

'Where are you phoning from?'

'Paris.'

'So are we going to meet?'

Christ, that was quick! I said, looking from Per to Jeanette and back again. Jeanette threw a cursory smile my way but I could see the conversation was all between Per and Jeanette now. I could have got up and left. Jeanette spoke again.

You glanced at me to check I was okay with Tina visiting. Maybe you wanted me to decide. Was that it?

Not really. Anyway, all you did was nod every time I looked to you for help or some kind of suggestion.

I felt she was your daughter and it was your call. Besides, I couldn't see any harm in her coming.

Per snorted at that and, with a quick glance at me, resumed his account.

So Tina replied, 'Sure. I'd like to meet you.' And I said, 'Well, clearly you know where we live . . . Why don't you come and stay for a few days? We don't have anything planned.' Jeanette just beamed, as if she found the whole thing hilarious.

No, not hilarious, Jeanette said. But Tina sounded so brash, so fresh: I was curious to meet her. And there was something else . . . I think maybe I liked the idea of someone we basically didn't know coming to stay. Life can get a bit stale as you get older. The spontaneity of our invitation and her acceptance recalled my youth, those shared houses where people – strangers – were always turning up, staying, then vanishing as inexplicably as they appeared.

Per nodded.

So I said to Tina, 'Just let us know when you're coming. We'll pick you up.' And Tina said, 'Great. I'll come by train.'

'When?'

'Tomorrow evening?'

At this point, Per stalled and Jeanette prompted him again: 'How will I recognize you?' you said.

That's right. And Tina replied, quick as an eel: 'Just look for my mother, the way she looked when you met her, and you'll find me. The only thing I ever got from you, Mum always says, is your skill at improvisation.'

'Really? You're musical?'

'Not in the slightest. I just improvise.'

And that was it, Per said, looking at me, as if he'd just remembered I was there, then back at his wife as if to confirm I might as well not be. Jeanette puffed on her cigar.

Wow, I muttered, reaching for a cliché: Quite a bombshell!

Absolutely, Per said, getting up and making for the toilet.

Jeanette's mouth was contorted in a gesture of evident demurral.

As the toilet door clicked shut on Per, I caught Jeanette's eye: What? You weren't that surprised? I asked.

Not really, no. After all, I'm the infertile one. And Per was always a frisky little rabbit. So it was on the cards, wasn't it? I'm sure you can remember the way things were in those days: men took no responsibility. If a woman wasn't on the pill, it was her look-out.

How could I not remember? Jeanette had had an abortion early in our relationship. It had been as much my fault as hers.

Neither of us had felt ready to have a child. There was nothing to say about it. I figured there never had been. If that abortion had resulted in infertility, I hadn't known it. I returned to the subject at hand.

So you never knew about his affair in Sheffield – if that's what it was?

Hell, no, Jeanette replied. He was away for months on end. I had an affair too while he was away. Several, actually.

So did Tina come?

Oh! Sure, Jeanette said, looking up as Per returned to the dining table: Wolf was just asking whether Tina ever turned up.

Grunting as he sat down, Per turned to his wife: Why don't *you* tell Wolf what happened when Tina arrived?

Okay, Jeanette said. But I'll tell it my way, all right?

Sure, Per said.

*

Jeanette went to the kitchen, returning with a bottle of whisky, a jug of water and three glasses. She poured the whisky, lit another Toscanello, held it away from her to examine the lit end, then took a deep breath.

Tina had my attention – Jeanette began – from the first moment I heard her on the telephone. Let me explain. My English isn't so good. I never passed any time in Sheffield or anywhere else abroad. But I heard the young woman's mood, I heard her anger. Do you know what I'm saying?

I'm not sure, I said.

A woman can often feel empathy for another woman's anger, right? Especially if the anger is directed at a man. But in Tina's case, I couldn't tell where the anger came from. So I was intrigued. I figured it really had nothing to do with Per. So I felt protective. What had he actually done to anyone that was so bad? Tina's mother had got pregnant and chosen to have a child? Good for her. Tina had got to have a life. Great. Also, I could see how excited Per was to be meeting his daughter. Elated. Euphoric. He had a child at last! And for free! He hadn't needed to change nappies, lose sleep, worry about school results, deal with adolescent sulks and inappropriate boyfriends, or become an unpaid taxi-driver for an ungrateful teenager . . . He was dreaming of having a fully formed child, the fruit of his younger loins, come home to embrace him. Am I exaggerating?

Per stared at his shoes. Well, a bit, he said.

Okay, a bit. Anyway, Tina showed up and was charming – especially to me . . .

Per snorted again and said, To me she was polite – at least to start with – but unswervingly distant. Do you remember? Before I'd even told her your name, she'd kissed *you* on both cheeks – the English never used to kiss strangers – but, when it came to greeting me, English reserve kicked right back in with a vengeance: she shook my hand, keeping me at arm's length, and clenched her teeth.

Yuh, Jeanette said again . . . For about thirty-six hours, it was like having a paying guest – except we were the ones doing the paying. We showed her the city, treated her to meals in restaurants, got an extra ticket so she could come to the opera with us. I have to say I found her great company. She told me about the books she was reading, including a lot of the second-wave feminist classics I'd read at college myself. In fact, she reminded me a lot of myself at that age. All this time not a word about the reason she'd come. But little by little she seemed to be thawing out with Per. They seemed almost relaxed together.

Then, on the third day, over breakfast, we stumbled somehow into the conversation we had all been waiting for and also postponing.

We didn't stumble, Per said. I asked her point-blank if she had a photo of her mum. I was expecting her to show me something recent on her smartphone but, no, she ran upstairs and came back with an old-fashioned hardback diary, which she opened and shook till some photos fluttered out.

This is my mum, she said, showing me one of a woman with a baby at her breast. Everything in that photo was utterly beautiful: the woman, the baby, the breast. I was taken aback. 'I don't recall her at all,' I said, transfixed.

'Well, you wouldn't, would you?' Tina snapped, snatching the photo from under our gaze: 'You were drunk. It was after a jazz gig. In Barnsley.'

Per didn't reply so I turned to Tina and said: 'Men get drunk sometimes. So do women. That happens. It isn't a crime.'

'Anyway,' Tina went on, addressing Per now. 'Mum took you back to her place in Sheffield and you had . . . sex. You weren't very interested and far too drunk to be any good. Don't look offended. She refused to tell me anything about the night I was conceived till I was seventeen and then she told me the whole damn thing, blow by blow. No finesse, she said. No warmth.' At that, both Tina and Per looked at me – as if for some kind of casting vote. I looked as blank as I could. I wasn't going to take sides.

'Why are you so angry with me?' Per then said. 'Because your mother thought I was a lousy lay when drunk? Or because I was never around when you were growing up? How could I have been? I didn't know I had a daughter. Maybe if your mother had thought to contact me . . .' At that, Tina erupted, jumped up and paced the floor. 'I didn't need a father. I had – and have – a perfectly good father. His name is Malcolm and he's been living with my mother since I was four. They're even married.' Tina picked another of the photos that had cascaded out of her diary and shoved it under our noses. 'See?' The new photo showed a man my age, my height, my girth, with a full beard just like mine.

Yuh, it was creepy, Jeanette said, lifting the whisky and gesturing towards my empty glass. I shook my head and covered the glass with my left palm.

So, Per said, I asked Tina again: 'Listen . . . Why are you so angry? From what you're saying, your mother and I had consensual sex. You were conceived. She never told me. What did I do wrong?' Tina replied: 'My mother went to a lot of trouble to put herself in your way. She'd been hanging around you for weeks, really fancied you, and you never noticed her. Even when she got you into bed, you were barely interested and you never tried to see her again. You don't even remember her, do you?'

'Are you telling me that your mother felt or feels hurt or insulted by me?'

'No,' Tina said, 'I'm telling you that I do.'

I could have laughed at that – it seemed so absurd – but the young woman had tears in her eyes.

Jeanette and Per stared at each another, unsmiling. Each seemed to be waiting for the other to continue. Then, with a glance, they seemed to agree it was Jeanette's turn.

After breakfast, Tina offered to leave, if we could just drive her to the station. We hesitated, then said she didn't have to go and that we were happy to spend the day at the coast as planned. To our surprise, she decided to stay. The rest of the day was filled with false smiles and inconsequential niceties, as if we'd signed a pact of non-aggression. We had a long, long walk. It was entirely relaxed and hypocritical. Which was fine. Just what we needed.

That seemed to be the end of the story. Per and Jeanette were both looking at me. I racked my brains for an appropriate comment.

Well, it's almost a happy ending, I said: father and daughter reunited, not exactly reconciled, but still.

I figured it was time for me to leave. I started to get up but then Per pulled a face, waving at me to sit back down. Oh god, there's more, I thought.

That evening, Per said, we went to bed straight after dinner, exhausted no doubt by the sea air. The following morning we drove Tina to the station. On the platform, as the train drew in, she turned to me and, as if delivering a prepared speech, yet twitching with nerves, said, 'I've had a great stay and it's been really interesting to meet someone my mother once slept with.' I wasn't paying attention to her choice of expression and even if I had been I might have let it go, but Jeanette protested at once. '"Someone your mother once slept with?" Is that it? Look, Tina. Per has done nothing wrong and he is, after all, your biological father.' 'Well, actually, no, he isn't,' Tina retorted, her eyes darting to left and right. 'I've been fibbing from the start. Mum got pregnant all right but decided to abort. She didn't think his genes were worth preserving. I was born about two years later.

Malcolm is my biological father.' 'Then why the anger?' Jeanette asked. 'Because he broke my mother's heart,' Tina said.

Per and I were so dumbfounded all we could do was wave her goodbye.

What else were we going to do? Per said.

I now lifted my glass and held it out for Jeanette to fill.

So, tell me Per, I said: How does it feel to discover you're a father, meet your supposed child, be insulted and humiliated, and then find she's not 'yours' after all? It must have been bewildering.

I was relieved, Per said. Sad, then relieved. How could I not be? She clearly didn't like me. I didn't much like her. Too mixed up, too bitter. Frankly, it was good to know she wasn't my flesh and blood and that her blue eyes and fair hair – common enough features, after all, in these latitudes – had nothing to do with me. Right from the start, I had no fatherly feelings towards her and I still can't recall a thing about her mother. No, I was glad to discover there was nothing between us.

Well, all's well . . . I said, glancing at my watch.

Neither of them took my cue.

Per settled back, seeming to sink into a dream.

Then Jeanette turned to Per.

I wouldn't be so certain there's nothing between you and Tina, she said, speaking so softly it was as though she weren't quite sure she wanted to be heard.

At first Per said nothing. It took a while for Jeanette's words to sink in. Then, sitting up a little straighter, he said: What do you mean?

Jeanette put down her glass.

We know Tina lied, don't we? That much is obvious. But do we know *when*?

Per's face enacted the dawning of a poisonous notion. Well, he flannelled, people sometimes lie out of sheer laziness. That's why I lie, when I lie. But then she's not like me, is she?

Jeanette spelled it out: If Tina was born two years later than she originally told us, she'd be little over eighteen now. Does she look eighteen? She said she was about to start her third year at college. That's a bit precocious even for a twenty-year-old. But for an eighteen-year-old? And she told me so much about her course work, the essays she's written, the dissertation she's working on. Could she make all that up? Anyhow, what about her touring Scotland in a campervan the summer before last? Since when can you drive in Britain at sixteen?

I see, Per said, putting down his whisky. His right arm was trembling. I glanced at his eyes. Then I saw that Jeanette was beaming in what looked like triumph. I suddenly felt I was intruding on some obscure and ugly power play. This had nothing to do with me, did it? I had no business being there.

I drained my whisky and got up. Per coughed and said I should come again next time I was in Copenhagen. Sure, I said. Jeanette showed me to the door.

*

Outside, in the breeze, Jeanette said it had been good to see me.

I stared up and down the street for a reply. If I hadn't had the whisky, maybe I would have censored my thoughts better, or at least my words.

Do you ever wonder, I blurted, how things might have been if we'd stayed together?

Never, Jeanette replied. Do you?

No, I said – a finger tugging at the lower eyelid of my left eye – neither do I.

I didn't love you, she said impatiently. I'm sure I must have told you that.

Actually, you told me the precise opposite. I've never forgotten your words: 'I do love you but Per needs me. You don't.'

I was probably lying to be kind.

To be kind? I repeated.

Unlike Tina, Jeanette added.

Unlike Tina? I don't follow.

Tina could have said she was born *one* year later. That would have been a bit of a stretch but plausible. But she had to say two, didn't she? She wanted us to figure it out. That was cruel.

But Per hadn't figured it out.

No. That's true.

So why did you have to force it on him? Was *that* kind?

It's important we live in truth.

Ha! But only when it suits you . . .

I waited and waited but Jeanette only smiled. I walked away. Neither of us said 'good night.'

*

I went back to my room at the university. I felt angry with just about everyone: with Tina for being a new-model puritan, with Per for being a softy, with Jeanette for being cruel, with myself for . . . what? For ever having loved Jeanette? The worst of it was that there had been some kind of psychodrama and I'd allowed myself to be sucked in.

My mobile rang. As I entered the building, I had switched it back on.

Hi, darling, my wife said. Your phone has been off all evening.

Yuh, I er . . . switched it off.

So where have you been?

I looked up an old flame.

Ah-ha.

And her husband.

So . . .

I probably told you about her years ago. Jeanette.

The one who lived in Copenhagen? The frigid one?

Jesus! I never said that, did I?

Whatever. Actually you did. Was it fun seeing her again?

Not exactly, no. In fact not at all.

Tell me about it. What happened? You sound so strange . . .

There's nothing to tell. I'm fine. Really.

There must be something. After all these years.

No, darling. There's nothing to tell. Really nothing at all.

Honestly?

I laughed at that, laughed harder than I'd expected.

Sure, I said. Honestly.

American Shades

THOSE DAYS, DURING daylight hours you might – at a cursory glance – mistake Bordeaux for a calm and happy city but, dwelling near its centre as we did, no such illusions were possible. It was a city of extremes: poor and wealthy neighbourhoods abutted one another, spawning contempt, envy, and violence. Sylviane and I worked and studied hard, yet occasionally still had time to kill and always energy to burn: we were young back then.

Frequently at night we were woken by brawling gangs of youths who would chase one another through the streets and alleys, and circle the little square on which our fourth-floor studio flat was situated, giving us an upper-circle view onto their running battles. Sometimes, long after the storm had moved off for its bloody climax elsewhere, we were woken again by swirling distant police sirens, an echo and a reminder, never altogether reassuring. Stepping out onto the pavement in the morning, we would sashay between the flecks and pools of blood that recorded the night just passed.

On one occasion, at around four in the morning, a saloon car screeched to a halt across the street. Kneeling at our window, we watched two men unload a body from the boot. They propped it against the wall then spat, as if making a statement of enduring importance. The driver glanced at the palm of his right hand, before wiping it on his trousers with a downward, forceful, smearing motion. We had no telephone of course – besides, who would we have called? The police? No, no: we returned shivering to bed and hugged each other all the closer.

One unusually peaceful night, we were woken by the sound of smashing bottles and whooping jollity – almost yodelling – from the small square below. We knew at once it was Jean-Luc. Who else would throw two bottles each time, one after the other at precisely calculated, ever varying, intervals – as if taking part in an impromptu percussion workshop. I pulled on my pyjamas and a coat. Sylviane yawned, dragged a pillow over her head, and said, *'Laisse-le faire, chéri'* 'No,' I said. 'Last time, he carried on for hours. Something has unsettled him. I'll go down and find out.'

Jean-Luc was surprised to see me but just nodded and went on throwing wine bottles at the wall, two by two, timed to hit and shatter separately, while I stood and looked around for a couple of minutes: he had another thirty-three lined up behind him. I began to count them down lazily: thirty-one, twenty-nine, twenty-seven . . . The pavement was strewn with broken glass and ran with pungent vinegary dregs.

'You okay?' I asked, when he glanced my way. 'Sure,' he said, pausing for breath. 'Isn't it a great sound?' 'You bet,' I said.

I surveyed the square. A couple of lights were lit in stray apartments, and through some half-open third-floor shutters an aged prostitute could be glimpsed leaning on her sill, cigarette clipped between index and middle fingers.

Jean-Luc threw another bottle, exulting again in the crashing and tinkling.

'You know, a lot of people like to sleep at night,' I observed, matter of fact, as he bent to pick up another brace of bottles. He looked surprised, as if I'd reminded him of something he'd long known but recently mislaid.

'Were *you* sleeping?' he asked, looking at the line of standing bottles, hesitant now.

'Well, yes. It's past three a.m. Are you sure you're okay?'

'Three a.m.?' he said slowly, as if the term required some deciphering.

Then he gave me his filthy right hand to shake, nodded like a bashful boy, and shuffled away, piping a tune. From across the square, I heard a shutter being closed and fastened. The catch made a metallic squeaking sound. I recall not looking up.

For about a year, we saw Jean-Luc most days, either on the street or when he rang our doorbell. We'd then hear his bright whistle circling in the echoing stairwell. As he reached the fourth landing, he'd tap on our open door, poke his head round, and say, '*Je peux?*' He'd shake my hand and give Sylviane a kiss on each cheek, then look for my guitar. Mostly he arrived while we were eating, but he refused all food, and would take only weak black tea with sugar. Within three months of meeting him, we found we had carpet fleas and head lice. We dealt with these inconveniences and made no mention of them to Jean-Luc, who continued to drop round as before. We always looked forward to his visits.

Jean-Luc was unlike any other *clochard* we'd ever met. He didn't drink alcohol, didn't smell of ancient urine, didn't fight, didn't beg for money – indeed, when handed money unsolicited, would pass it on to the next person he encountered or leave it on a convenient ledge. I never saw him ask anybody for anything except, once or twice, a cigarette paper, which he'd then fill with tobacco scavenged from discarded dog-ends. Nor did he take any drugs – unless you count the occasional spliff. Sylviane and I used to have grass from time to time and we always offered to share with him, but he rarely accepted and only then, it seemed, as a matter of etiquette.

What we enjoyed most about his visits were his musicianship and his conversation. Most people, on picking up a guitar, play recognisable tunes or at least chords you've heard before. Not Jean-Luc. Using his own seemingly infinite set of tunings, he produced a rhythmic stream of melodies and harmonies that were completely unpredictable and yet strangely compelling, even easy on the ear. When he put the guitar down, usually to smoke or to sip at his tea, he would spin the strangest stories or lay out the oddest theories you ever could hope to hear. Everything was different with Jean-Luc, experimental, tentative, fresh-minted.

Once I picked up the guitar just after he'd left our flat and attempted to play a snatch of 'Jean-Luc music' but I couldn't come close: my fingers just fell back into timeworn patterns and shapes. And whenever I tried to jot down from memory any of his talk, by the very next day none of it made any sense. Yet as long as he was playing or speaking, you'd listen, hanging on each note or word, as if on the brink of some resounding, perhaps final soundscape, or even truth.

It occurred to us much later that we knew little about Jean-Luc. He had once mentioned a brother, another time described an industrial accident in vivid detail. We put two and two together and concluded his brother had been maimed or maybe killed in a factory and that he had seen it happen. But when we tried to learn more, he evaded us, chuckled, began again to speak in his gnomic or cryptic way or reached for the guitar, retuning it incessantly. I suppose Jean-Luc's obsession with tunings served to ensure that he would never play the same thing twice.

About the most coherent thing I ever heard Jean-Luc say was on the topic of 'difference.' I think I'd remarked, probably quite lamely, that he wasn't like other people. He paused a moment then looked at me with something like pity and said – and I jotted this down as soon as he left and put it in my diary that evening: 'But difference, difference from other people is easy: everybody is more or less different from everybody else. It's being different from yourself, resolutely different, day in day out, minute by minute, stubbornly at one remove from yourself, as if stepping outside your own skin and thoughts: now, that's a trick worth having.'

Mostly when we encountered Jean-Luc in the city he was alone, walking, walking, walking, apparently with a purpose, seeming always to be searching for something. He'd told us about the restaurants, hotels, upscale condominiums, and smart parks he knew. He lived from bins, was familiar with all the best ones and knew precisely when to check them. Very occasionally we'd see him in the company of other *clochards*, but only ever at the edge of a group, talking quietly to one or at most two people. If there was a guitar, he would be playing it, or waiting his turn.

The very first time we'd noticed Jean-Luc, he was sitting in Place St.-Pierre alongside two other men, a pair of inseparable *clochard* old-timers, one very tall and the other very short, and Jean-Luc was playing a battered old Eco missing the D and B strings. 'Tall' and 'Short' – as Sylviane and I soon learnt to call them – were silent, gazing moodily in opposite directions, as if they had recently argued. The moment we heard the sounds Jean-Luc conjured from that miserable instrument, we stopped and listened. When he put the guitar down to roll a cigarette, he acknowledged our presence and we engaged him in conversation. I said I had an old Yamaha twelve-string and told him our address but he knew nothing of streets or square names so we walked him there and invited him to drop in at any time. I showed him our names on the door bell. He smiled at us in turn, held out his filthy hand to shake, and said he would come by. Then he vanished.

For several months during that winter of '79, we saw Jean-Luc almost every day, in the street or in our flat. Then, as spring came and we got busier with work and exam preparation, he called on us less often. We lent him the guitar one time, but when he brought it back a machine-head was damaged and a deep swerving gash had somehow been scoured alongside the bridge.

In early May, he briefly went missing. At first we thought he might simply have stopped calling on us so, every evening, we wandered through the city looking for him. At last we found Tall and Short sheltering from a squall in Place St.-Michel. We asked them at once whether they'd seen Jean-Luc. They seemed surprised. It was as if they hadn't noticed his absence. When we asked them where he might possibly be, they performed a collaborative shrug and Tall held out his palm. However, even with money in it, he had nothing to tell us.

After two weeks' absence, Jean-Luc rang our bell and came straight up, looking tanned and rested. 'Where have you been?' we asked, once he'd kissed Sylviane and shaken my hand. 'I wanted to see the sea,' he said. 'So where did you go?' 'Lacanau,' he said, naming the nearest resort, forty kilometres away. 'I walked there and I walked back,' he added. 'Where did you sleep? What did you eat?' I asked. Jean-Luc laughed. 'I ate just anywhere, anything. I slept whenever and wherever I needed. I'm free, you know.' 'We missed you,' Sylviane then said. I nodded hard. Jean-Luc seemed surprised and touched. He played for hours that day and before he left he said, 'I'll always be here, you know. I never go any distance and I never stay away long. These are my streets. This city is my home. Should you ever wish to find me, come to these streets and within a few hours or days – this side of death – you'll see me coming round a corner.'

That summer it was Sylviane and I who decided to leave the city, and for good. We realized immediately that Jean-Luc was the person we'd miss most. He was in our flat playing the guitar when we told him what we were planning. He stopped, mid-phrase, looked at us in astonishment, and said, 'What's the point? Elsewhere is just the same as here. Leaving is the same as staying.' We had no explanation. We were restless, we said, and we thought we'd be happier elsewhere. He shook his head, just two sharp jerks. It was a gesture we'd never seen him perform, and never saw again.

The day we left Bordeaux, we searched high and low for Jean-Luc. We'd said goodbye to everyone else. In the end, with heavy hearts, we asked the various *clochards*, including Tall and Short, to say goodbye to Jean-Luc for us, and to give him our best wishes. 'Sure,' they said, their hands reaching out. 'Sure,' they repeated, less persuasively, once we'd given them coins.

Over the next several years, we returned many times to Bordeaux, first to tie up loose ends at the university, later to see Sylviane's family. Each time we returned, we went looking for Jean-Luc and sooner or later found him, just as he had promised, coming round some corner or sitting, usually on his own, on some street or square. We thought he grew thinner and his hair certainly began to go white. He always recognised us and seemed pleased and quickly asked if we would stay this time. But each time we had to tell him we wouldn't be staying and then the conversation sputtered and died.

Of those final meetings with Jean-Luc just two stand out: one toward the end of winter '82, the other in summer '85. After that, I didn't return to Bordeaux until the early years of the new millennium when, now on my own, I searched for him for several days, picturing him weather-beaten and white-haired. I found no trace. 'This side of death . . .' he'd promised. I had to assume he had crossed over.

So the last time I saw Jean-Luc was in the summer of '85. I found him in the company of Short, whom I recognised at once – Tall, it seemed, was no longer around. Jean-Luc was quieter than I had ever known him. He had lost his smile, seemed stunned somehow, though he greeted me quite warmly and gave me his hand to shake. I asked him for his news but he only shook his head. Short launched into a rambling story about how they and other *clochards* had been bundled into a van one day and driven to a psychiatric facility where for several weeks they'd been experimented on. Within a matter of days, most people were thinking they were Jesus, Lenin, Che or Napoleon. Mostly Jesus. 'Who did *you* think you were?' I asked, turning to Jean-Luc. Jean-Luc looked at me in surprise, then glanced at Short, who said, 'Him? He never had any doubts. He was himself. It was other people who thought Jean-Luc was Jesus.'

Jean-Luc laughed at this, his eyes twinkling, mischievous. 'Do you know who was the very first nut, the very first fraud, ever to claim he was the son of God? No? Because, you know, nuts have been making these claims for years, centuries. Can't you guess who was the first one?' I shrugged, playing along, trying to guess the 'correct' answer. 'You give in?' 'Sure,' I said. 'It was Jesus himself. And if Jesus *wasn't* the first nut to claim he was Christ, he was certainly the first nut to make himself a name for doing so.'

But it is the earlier encounter, back in the winter of '82, that comes to mind more often.

It was a bright February day when I bumped into Jean-Luc, on his own this time, in Cours Alsace-Lorraine. He was sitting on a step, playing with a pair of mirror-lens sunglasses, a style that was popular at the time. One of the arms was broken and one of the lenses cracked, but they still 'worked' – more or less. Jean-Luc was clearly delighted with them, putting them on and taking them off, striking poses, even using the mirrors as mirrors occasionally. He'd found them that very morning, he informed me.

I had noticed at once that Jean-Luc's left cheek was bruised and the skin beneath his right eye was yellowed. Also, his upper lip had been broken and a scab had formed right in the middle of it. And he kept sucking on one of his teeth. Probably it hurt.

'What happened to you?' I asked, sitting down beside him and giving him my hand. 'Nothing,' he said, glancing up the street.

'You look like you've been in a fight,' I said.

'Nobody fights me – they'd be too scared,' he said, sounding serious. I considered his slight stature and brittle-looking frame and chuckled briefly.

'So what happened?' I asked.

A confused story emerged. A bevy of Paris dignitaries – politicians and town planners, mostly – had decided to make a lightning official visit to the city. The police had rounded up all the tramps and hobos, driving them fifty kilometres out of town in a couple of vans, then pushing them out at the side of the road and telling them to find their own way back. By the time they made it to the city, the dignitaries had seen what they wanted to see and decamped back to Paris.

'But why did they hit you?' I asked Jean-Luc. Jean-Luc shrugged and put the mirror shades on and shook his locks in the hippie manner.

'Did they hit everybody?' I asked. Again, Jean-Luc shrugged. It irritated me. 'How can they behave like that? It must surely be illegal . . .'

Jean-Luc could see I was angry, scandalised, agitated.

He took the sunglasses off and put them back on again several times, glancing in the mirror lenses occasionally to check his own appearance. He waited till I had finished fuming, then smiled at me and said:

'*Écoute. C'est rien. C'est juste le tarif pour ceux qui portent les lunettes américaines.*' Listen, it's nothing, it's just the price you pay for wearing American shades.

Dead and Alive

One.

Western Ukraine, 24 September 2015

Dear Clive,

This will be my first and final letter. I look forward to hearing from you – just once, as agreed. I trust my family, former husband, etc. have not reacted too badly. But in any case, there's no way back for me now. I hope you found the classic brown envelope I pushed through your letter box on my drive down to Cornwall. It should more than cover any costs you have incurred.

This is just to confirm that everything went to plan and the P.O. box address I gave you is still valid. That evening, I parked the car in the clifftop carpark, leaving the back seat strewn with old clothes, bits and pieces of supermarket snacks, and an almost empty bottle of gin. No note. Instead, I left a message on my sister's voicemail ('Tell everyone I'm sorry.'), then called you. I dumped the phone on the passenger seat, beside the car keys.

The boat was late coming but I wasn't worried. I knew I could count on Inna. It was a cloudy and moonless night, pitch dark, warm even for mid-September. The sea was calm. It was just before two a.m. when I heard Inna's voice. I suppose I had drifted off to sleep. She'd swum ashore in a leotard, leaving the boat circling just beyond the breakers in the capable hands of Jannsens, a genial Flemish racketeer who owed her a favour.

Inna hugged and kissed me, showering me in salt. I think she was more excited than I was. I undressed, leaving everything but my underwear just above the high-tide line, then we swam out to the boat. I hadn't the strength to haul myself aboard. It was a good thing Jannsens was there to help me. Inna had thought of everything, including a dry set of clothes, hot soup, and Calvados.

It was 'plain sailing' indeed: a westerly breeze sprang up at about five, just after sunrise. Inna and I had talked for hours, then gone below deck and slept. Jannsens brought us in to land the following evening around ten p.m., just south of Brest. It was Sunday and there wasn't a soul in sight. Inna's car was parked nearby. The first thing she did was show me my new identity documents: henceforth I was a New Zealander. I felt then that 'Jamie' was dead and that I was being reborn. From Brittany to Inna's home just outside Lviv, we drove well over two thousand kilometres. We had to display identity papers only twice. God bless Europe!

That's all there is to tell. I'm grateful to you, Clive, really I am. If you're ever in our part of the world, have a great time. But please don't look me up. I'm dead and intend to stay that way. Have a good life.

'Jamie'

Two.

Chichester, England.
3 October 2015

Dear Jamie (since I have no other name for you),

I must congratulate you. When you first told me of your plan, though I recognized at once that it could work, I have to say I doubted your determination to see it through. Even after you revealed to me the depths of your disillusion with your home, friends, and family, I still didn't believe you were prepared to slam the door on your past life. I now know how wrong I was. You're one of the most resolute and rational people I've ever met and I salute you for it.

Anyway, that's enough of that: compliments are for Americans, as some famous author once wrote. The deal was that I would contact you just once – to report on the reactions of your erstwhile loved ones to what they take to be your self-administered watery death.

By the time the memorial service was held – on the Thursday, ten days after you disappeared – the media had moved on to a story about a kidnapped child. The police had of course contacted the usual experts on marine currents, etc., and had issued a statement that if, as had to be assumed, you had swum out from where your clothes had been recovered and then got into difficulties, your body might not be found for a very long time, if ever. Julian, your therapist for over a year (a nice touch, that . . .) had contacted the police and confirmed that you'd been receiving CBT for compulsive gambling and had recently shared with him your thoughts of suicide. I of course relayed the details of our final 'unsettling' conversation. I told them I thought I'd managed to talk you out of it. Your sister told them of the voicemail she received the night you vanished.

Thus far nobody seems to have suspected any form of foul play. You'd emptied your bank accounts rather erratically over the previous months, you'd remade your will, bequeathing everything to your family except for a small donation to Gamblers Anonymous. It all seemed open and shut: a sad case but somehow inconsequential. A lonely old woman kills herself – don't hold the front page!

The ceremony was low-key. Everybody who attended found something or other to say. Most expressed surprise but not, as it were, alarm. I had a discreet digital recording device in my shirt pocket. The sound quality is not great but it helps to jog my memory. After all, who wouldn't want an accurate account of their own memorial service?

I recognized your mother as soon as she stood up to speak.

Your description of her was spot-on. She sparkled from her blonde highlights down her crushed silk dress all the way to her patent leather high heels. She kept it brief and dignified, saying that you had always been the perfect daughter, that she had loved you dearly, even if you had never been as close as some mothers and daughters, and that in any case she would never get over your loss. She raised a hand to her eye but then lowered it again, either because there was in fact no tear to wipe away or because she feared for her makeup.

Your daughter told us about your gambling habits. Apparently, she said, you had taken to frequenting the seedier southern coastal resorts, spending entire days gambling at the lower end of the market, addicted even, she reported with a grimace, 'to end-of-the-pier one-arm bandits.' More than anything else she sounded ashamed of you. Well, you did ask me to be honest. As she sat down, she added, apparently as an afterthought, that you'd been 'a perfectly adequate mother.' Not quite a ringing endorsement.

Your sister talked next. She took up where your daughter left off, describing your childhood in Southend and suggesting that your 'recourse' to 'downmarket seaside resorts' was some kind of throwback. Then, speaking in that thin sharp voice of hers, she said – and here I can quote verbatim, because everyone fell silent and my DRD picked up every word: 'As a feminist, I'm both surprised and disappointed by Jamie's decision to take her own life. Men you rather expect to kill themselves if things go awry: they realize how inessential they are, how dispensable. Sometimes all it takes is for them to get jilted at an awkward age (fourteen? forty-nine? seventy-seven?), lose their job-for-life, get caught with their hand rather too publicly in the till or in their zipper, or are suddenly bereaved, abandoned by a lifelong companion or see their mutt run over. Almost anything can do it. They lose a will to live that was never very strong to begin with. You come to expect it of them. But not of women. I feel, frankly, as much disappointment as sorrow. I feel Jamie has let all of us women down. You might not like to hear this but it needed to be said.'

Beryl spoke next. She was all choked up, just as you said she would be. Holding back the tears, she said, 'Jamie and I have been . . . must I really now say, *had* been? . . . good friends for over fifty years. Ever since school we always told each other everything. Or at least I thought we did. I believed we were each other's lifelong confidante. Jamie brought me her troubles, I brought her mine. I see now that over the years our friendship had shrunk to that. When we were happy and fine we didn't talk much – let alone meet. Lately, I'd heard from her rather infrequently. I assumed that everything was okay. Her suicide makes no sense to me. How can you kill yourself when you're somebody's mother, daughter, ex-wife, sister, line manager, dependable neighbour, reliable friend? It's so sad. I wish she had told me how desperate she was feeling. For she must have been feeling desperate – mustn't she? – to do such a thing . . . If only she had called me . . . I feel sure I could have found the right words to dissuade her.'

Beryl hesitated an instant before swallowing hard and adding, 'But we must try to be positive. To honour Jamie's memory. That's what we're here for, aren't we? To celebrate her life? Well, I shall remember Jamie as a kind and lovely person, a great conversationalist despite her shyness, a linguist, and a connoisseur of the art world. And always ready for an adventure. After we both retired, we went on several city breaks together – Lisbon in February, Tallinn in November, you know the kind of thing. It made us feel young again. We liked to flirt with the other group members or the tour guides. Jamie could still turn a head. It was a lot of fun. *She* was a lot of fun.'

'Our last trip was to Bruges. On the second evening, we stumbled into a gay bar just across the road from our hotel, not realizing at first quite where we were. A tall blonde late-middle-aged woman approached us and we fell into conversation. She said she was attending an international conference of high-ranking police administrators. She was from somewhere in Eastern Europe. She claimed to be an investigator. It was fascinating. This woman – Ukrainian or Belarusian, I seem to remember – told the most amazing stories of organized crime and its connections with governments and corporations. Nothing incriminating, let alone self-incriminating, of course. She was quite a character.'

'Anyway, I couldn't keep up with Jamie on the vodka, had never quite possessed her stamina in that or in any other department, so I made my excuses and went back to our hotel. I felt a bit bad leaving her there, but Jamie smiled and waved me away and the Eastern European police person – if that's truly who she was – said, 'Don't worry! I'm not going to rape her!' I thought that was a bit 'off' but Jamie roared with laughter and almost shooed me away! That's the last image I have of Jamie: sitting in a bar, talking to a complete stranger, drinking a little too much, laughing her head off, happy for all the world.' Beryl took a deep breath, then, trembling, said, 'I just wanted to share that image with you all.'

After Beryl sat down, the room remained very silent for what seemed a long time. I had muttered, 'how interesting,' but nobody else made any comment. It was as if they thought Beryl had talked out of turn in some way. Or perhaps nobody was really interested in what she had said. In any case, I really don't think you have anything to fear from Beryl's disclosure.

Next came some rather shorter contributions. Your neighbour said how much you had laughed together about your pets and their foibles and how she could always count on you for an onion, an egg or a slice of bread. Some man you once managed – David? – said in a fawning, awkward manner that you had possessed great 'nurturing skills.'

Then your ex-husband spoke. The way everyone glowered at him! I'd noticed earlier that your daughter had barely acknowledged his existence and that your mother, when he'd shambled in, had held out her hand and looked the other way while he pumped it. As if he had a disease or terrible breath. Stuttering slightly, he said that although it had hurt terribly at the time the kindest thing you ever did was to leave him. He said that if it hadn't been for your support he'd never have survived those first few months alone, nor managed to deal with his 'alcohol issues.' He told us what he was now doing and how he was feeling. He said he had developed an interest in genealogy and was learning to cook risottos. About you he said absolutely nothing.

Finally, it was my turn to speak. I stated, as you'd suggested, that we'd been close at university and that you'd found me online quite recently and that we'd met a couple of times, gone out a little, mostly to operas, and then drifted apart again. I said I'd always been fond of you and that I was sorry you had left us but that you had nonetheless had a good life and that we could and should celebrate that and respect your last decision. I didn't think I'd said anything controversial.

As I sat down, to my astonishment I saw your mother get up again. 'No, Clive. No, Beryl.' she snapped. 'That really won't do. If Jamie was such a good and lovely person, why has she now inflicted this insult on us? I have to say I take her act very personally and if she were here I would give her a piece of my mind. This disappearance, this suicide, whatever it is, may appear senseless, but when did Jamie do anything that wasn't carefully calculated? She will even have imagined this gathering. That's why I sense she is still with us. I can't believe she committed a desperate spur-of-the-moment act. Whatever else it was, it was ALSO – I'm sorry I have to repeat myself – a calculated insult hurled at all those who loved and cherished her.'

After your mother sat down, everyone except myself and Beryl filed past her – presumably to thank her for saying what she'd said. As I then walked away from the gathering, I sensed that your mother had found a way of settling almost everybody, reconciling them to what had happened, providing them with reassurance and 'closure,' furnishing a convenient narrative of your life in which you were cast as the villain and they were all off the hook.

That's all there is to say really. You were absolutely right. They will get along perfectly well without you. Beryl, of course, will miss you more than the others, but she too will get over it.

All that remains for me to say now is that I wish you a long and happy life. And – thanks for the brown envelope. It is very generous. But, to be frank, I would have helped you for nothing. You deserve to be free, you deserve a fresh start.

All the best,
Clive.

Three.

Julie – as she was now known – was sitting in a well-appointed and spacious living room in the house she now shared with Inna on the outskirts of Lviv. It was early evening. Inna had returned from work at the city police department, stopping on her way home to check for post at her P. O. box. She had found Clive's letter and, resisting every professional impulse, brought it back to Jamie unopened, handing it over discreetly and then going to her gym room, where she was now working out to a soundtrack of loud Ukrainian jazz-rock.

Julie finished reading the letter and laid it aside. She sighed with contentment, then thought, 'So what now?'

She picked up the diary she had begun shortly after meeting Inna in Bruges, almost two years earlier. She read the latest entry dated '5 October 2015. Lviv,' which began as follows: '"Jamie" is dead and buried. So long live Julie, the New Zealander.' There followed a very detailed account of her staged 'suicide,' her first impressions of Lviv, and so on. As she read it through, Julie felt that it was all too perfect, written in a mood that was cloyingly euphoric. She flicked back a few weeks, then a few months, then a year and a half. She came to rest at an entry dated '3 April 2014. Dresden.'

'I'm sitting at the airport. I've had the most amazing four days here with Inna. We've been everywhere and done everything – we even went to the opera to see a production of Janacek's *Jenufa*. Inna knows nothing of opera – or theatre or the arts in general or serious music – and it's a joy and a delight to initiate someone who has such open curiosity and who, owing to her background and career choices, has so much to learn; a whole new world is opening up to her and I'm to be her privileged and attentive guide. On the other hand, Inna knows Dresden really well, having studied here in the mid-'80s. She introduced me to friends from that time. Most of them were young apparatchiks in the old GDR state apparatus and some of them, she thinks, were Stasi members. Yet last night when they talked of the past, there was no hint of either guilt or nostalgia. I suppose they've all done pretty well for themselves since the wall came down. As has Inna, of course.'

'What began as an unexpected bi-curious fling has turned into true love. "True love" – it's a long time since I've heard that expression let alone used it myself in anything but derision. Personally, I never expected to love again. Or to be loved. And, miracle of miracles, it's clear that Inna feels the same way. She has said as much. I am almost embarrassed and ashamed at my happiness. Which is exactly what I told her yesterday evening, as we were in our hotel room getting ready to go out. She laughed and said "ashamed!?" and then scolded me for being "so terrifically English!" and said I should "seize the day." When we got back – slightly tipsy – I went online to find Andrew Marvell's "To His Coy Mistress" just to prove that English people too can be spontaneous, passionate, adventurous and "seize the day." She read the poem over and over and insisted I explain some of the words. Then she went very quiet and said, "In that case, if you're serious, I may have a plan."'

'We have already talked about living together eventually but she always refuses point-blank to uproot herself, give up work, move house. She told me when we met for that weekend in Paris that if anyone is to move, it will have to be me. When I replied that in any case I'm so tired of my life in England – there's really nothing to keep me there, not a single person I'd particularly miss or who needs me any longer, she seemed surprised. Then she said, "Besides, if you came to live with me, you could always travel home occasionally and keep in touch." I thought about that, then said, "I don't think I'd want to." "Are you afraid of coming out?" she then asked, rather pointedly. "Hell, no. The only aspect of coming out that would bother me is the excruciatingly boring need to do so. Why should one ever explain? I can already see the pinched faces of my mother, my sister, my neighbour, my few friends. I can just picture everybody scrambling to show how commendably tolerant, liberal and understanding they are . . ."'

'Anyway, last night, after reading Marvell's poem, Inna took a deep breath and laid out this audacious yet wonderfully simple plan. She was completely calm and completely rational and completely confident: "I know how everything relevant works: shipping, identity papers, police enquiries, borders . . . Believe me, it's one hundred percent feasible." I heard her out, then burst out laughing. "It would be *too* perfect," I said. "But I don't think I really have the courage. Unlike you, Inna, I've led a very safe life. I just don't do things like that. Nobody in my family has ever *vanished*." "Oh, well . . ." Inna said, shrugging. So that's how we've left it. I'm such a coward!'

Julie laughed and closed the diary. She noticed that the sound of Ukrainian jazz-rock had ceased. Inna was probably having a shower. She thought briefly of Inna's body, her heavy breasts and strong thighs, then pictured her face. She reopened her diary, took up her pen and wrote:

Lviv. 10 October 2015.
I received Clive's letter today. It's incredible. My mother and sister and everyone except Beryl – bless her – have found a very satisfactory way of dealing with my 'suicide': resentment! They feel I've insulted them! It could hardly be better. I feel vindicated. My only regret is Beryl: but, as Clive points out, she too will get over it. As for me, I don't think I'll miss any of the things or people I've left behind. Is that so terrible? Inna came into the kitchen the other day and tuned the radio into the BBC. A kind gesture? Or a test? I asked her to switch it off. The thing is: I don't want to hear the chimes of Big Ben, the Archers, the shipping forecast, the Moral sodding Maze, any of it. *This* is my home now. I've resolved to go completely native. I shall learn everything I need to know here by discarding all the baggage I no longer require. I shall learn to speak Ukrainian and at least to understand Russian. I've always been good at languages. It'll take time of course. I'm only sixty, Inna's just sixty-one. If I'm lucky I could have thirty years or more ahead of me. Here. Or maybe elsewhere. With Inna. Or maybe without Inna. I'm seizing that day.

This is my second life. After all, one life should never be enough for anyone. Some people – men, especially, but increasingly women too nowadays – get to live parallel lives: one at work, one at home; or one with the spouse, one with the lover; or one in Paris, one in London; or one during the week, another at the weekend; or one in the flesh, another online. Like most women, I got saddled at some point with a single, never-ending, monotonously spooling life, where work and home shaded seamlessly into each other, and colleagues, friends, and family – such as they were – became inextricably entangled, and all my leisure activities became merely functional, as if precisely designed to get me to work by eight a.m. Monday morning and back between the crisp conjugal sheets by eleven p.m. at night. Every little thing I did made perfect sense, and I was complete, wasn't I? If asked, anyone who knew me would have said that I possessed – horror of horrors – 'total integrity.' The truth is that for years, most of the time I felt like screaming.

I can hear Inna pottering about in the kitchen. I'm going to finish this paragraph now, close my diary till tomorrow – or maybe close it forever. Who knows? I began it when I met Inna but maybe I no longer need it.

My second life begins here. Down that corridor.

The Power of Reptiles

I'M EXHAUSTED, GINA muttered, struggling to rise from the sofa. Besides, there's nothing on TV.

In the corner of the kitchen, in half light, Gabriel was bent over a screen. He finished a sentence, pressed Enter, and waited.

I'm going up, Gina said. I've a long day teaching tomorrow.

Gabriel glanced at the winking cursor, waiting for the reply, then got to his feet. He took Gina in his long, large arms.

Don't go up yet, he pleaded. Wait for me. I just want to check they're all okay. There's been violence. It's not quite seven p.m. there. Carmen isn't back from work. Please. Don't go to bed without me. Ten minutes. I promise.

Gina sighed, lifted her head, and kissed Gabriel on the jaw. Then she returned to the lounge, poured a whisky, and slumped on the sofa. She was too tired to read even a newspaper. She clicked on the TV.

When they went to bed, Gabriel always needed to be held, otherwise he couldn't fall asleep without nightmares assailing him. Mostly he accepted this meant he had to go to bed whenever Gina wanted but, just occasionally, as tonight, when he was waiting for news from family, he begged her to wait. And she waited.

Gina had only the five old-fashioned terrestrial channels to choose from. They had tried cable, satellite, and various multi-channel packages, but had given up on all of them. Most evenings, they didn't watch TV at all. Gabriel found the best way to follow events at home in Caracas was to tune into local radio stations over the internet. When Gabriel was home, the house crackled and echoed to distant dramas and Latin American voices.

Gina listened with interest to all Gabriel's accounts of Venezuela and stories about his family but she'd never been across the Atlantic nor met any of them. Besides, Gabriel now had an excellent job with the BBC and seemed settled.

She savoured the whisky. Channel Five was on the last lap of one of its '100 greatest' programmes: tonight it was supermodels. Gina admired the leggy divas on the screen, feeling no envy, only curiosity. Kicking off her shoes and pulling her feet up under her, she sat back in judgement over the models' gaudy yet brittle appearance. She caught glimpses of their lives and dreamt she could imagine the rest.

Gabriel was using Messenger to 'talk' to his family in Venezuela. Some 'fucking bean-brain' of a US senator – as Gabriel described Pat Buchanan – had called for the President of Venezuela to be assassinated. It was a signal, Gabriel had said. It meant the US wanted regime change in Caracas and probably didn't care how. I mean, when did they ever . . .?

Gina kept an eye on the supermodels but her thoughts strayed to Gabriel's sister and mother, both precariously employed in Venezuela's capital city, and Raúl, Gabriel's uncle, who worked as a schoolteacher in a slum *barrio*. They had all welcomed the election of Chavez, and still hoped for better times. Gina and Gabriel had a running joke: since Chavez had promised that under his administration oil revenue would go to the needy, each time the price of petrol in London went up, Gina and Gabriel would comment wryly, Never mind – all the more for the folks back home!

A talking head from an ad agency was now telling an anecdote about Jerry Hall, whom she'd just referred to as the sexiest woman in the world. Gina – who was five foot four – looked at Jerry's endless bony legs and pinprick eyes, and shrugged. The Texan model had allegedly been asked how she held on to such a notoriously unfaithful man as Mick Jagger and she had allegedly replied, I give him a blowjob before he goes to work each morning.

In the darkness, over her whisky, Gina raised one eyebrow. She pictured the front door of an ordinary suburban English house, as filmed from the stairs. The model's lover was standing with his back against the door, holding a briefcase and staring fixedly, his eyes half-closed, his famous lips sagging, while his trousers lapped about his ankles. The supermodel, in full cat-walk regalia, was on her knees, her back to the camera, her head bobbingly engaged in her husband's crotch. Some commercials came on and Gina hit the remote.

ITV had a fly-on-the-wall documentary about a legal brothel in the US. Everything seemed so normal. The girls chatted about the peculiarities of the clients and the outlandishness of some of the services they requested. There was footage of a client being trampled by five of the girls, two in high heels. Over on BBC2 there was a discussion of Ethics and Religion, involving a Catholic bishop, a Rabbi and a Jain. The moderator said something about 'finding common ground' and the holy men grinned.

Everything okay, Gabriel? Gina shouted.

Yuh. I'm just, er, talking to Pedro. Things are calm. I'm, er, almost done. But there are rumours, tensions, you know.

Gina nodded like she knew, then took another sip. But all she knew of Gabriel's background was the little he told her. What mattered to Gina was how Gabriel was with her – kind and gentle and open: she knew that he loved her and she loved him back. On first meeting, neither of them had been looking for anything from anybody, both of them had been living contentedly with other people. But one moment they had been acquaintances, the next soul mates.

Channel Five still had commercials, but BBC1 was screening a wildlife programme about reptiles. Gina hated reptiles. Channel 4 had a Hollywood comedy starring Sandra Bullock. What a choice, Gina thought, Sandra Bullock or reptiles. Christ, late-night TV . . .

Back to the reptiles by mistake, then, via the religious talking heads, to another supermodel, someone from Brazil called Gisèle. There were glimpses of streets in Rio. It didn't look anything like downtown Caracas. But then why should it? It's the other end of the continent, isn't it? Bucharest probably doesn't look much like London. Or Tallinn.

Then back to the US brothel. What the hell was that? Gina wondered, her mouth falling open. The girls were standing round a mechanical contraption featuring a more than life-sized dildo protruding from a curved flank of what looked like solid steel. The brothel director, a buxom middle-aged woman who reminded Gina of a particular head teacher, was explaining how this 'female pleasurer' functioned. There were buttons you could press to adjust the swivel action and the vibration speed of the dildo. There was even a remote-control device. Some of the girls looked doubtful but the camera panned to two who giggled and pouted. Then the Madam called for a volunteer.

There was a moment's hesitation. Now, come on, don't be shy, she said. Then, in a tone that brooked no opposition: Suzy?

Gina could hardly believe what she was watching. I'd better have a stiff one, she decided, refilling her glass.

Suzy, the giggliest of all the girls, had gamely dropped her panties and was now straddling the machine. Her legs had to go up onto stirrup-like supports, reminding Gina of a recent visit to the gynaecologist: nothing to worry about. The camera focused on the protruding dildo as Suzy impaled herself upon it, whereupon both the dildo and Suzie's crotch melted into a patch of censorious knitting.

The camera switched avidly to the young woman's face. Suzy bit her lips very prettily and gasped very lasciviously. Her perfectly manicured right hand tweaked the nipple of her perfectly enhanced left breast. There was some eye-rolling from the other women while Suzy started to pant.

Flores and Alberta say hi!, Gabriel called from the next room.

Right! said Gina, Say hello from me. Say I'm thinking about them and really hope they manage to come soon.

She switched briefly to the reptiles, the supermodels, the ethics and the Sandra Bullock vehicle, but quickly returned to the brothel, where the scene had changed.

The Madam and the girls – including Suzy, who had now evidently dismounted the contraption, donned panties, and recovered her composure – were discussing the business potential of the 'pleasurer.'

I don't know if y'all realize how exciting our customers are gonna find this machine, the Madam said, looking around.

Hey, Georgie, you're looking downright mystified . . .

Georgie decided to speak her mind.

Well, I dunno, and maybe it's plain dumb of me, but, like, I can see us gals having some fun all right with this machine, when nobody's looking, but as for the clients . . . I mean . . . we don't get that many fags in here, now do we? So, excuse me but, what good is it to them?

There was a short-lived uproar of amused cackling, but the girls noticed the Madam wasn't laughing, and they all fell silent and, like novices, gazed up at her.

Let me put it like this: what is it men want? I mean: what really turns them on? she asked. Christ! Gina thought, that woman's a born teacher, she could run a damn school.

Being trampled? someone piped, not obviously joking.

Fine. Thank you for that, Lucy. But I'm not actually thinking of the guys who come here looking for pain and humiliation. Any ideas? No? No idea what men really get off on? Boy, you girls are green. Well, I'll tell you then. What really does it for men is control. Do you follow me? Control. So just imagine how much fun they'll have with one of you stuck on this machine and the remote control in their sweaty little hands? Let's face it, for most of them it's going be the first time they ever make a woman come. And just when they want to too! Because, as we witnessed and as Suzy can surely testify, this female pleasurer does what it says. Ain't that right, Suzy?

Suzy simpered. The commercials rolled.

Is everything okay, darling? Gina shouted. Yeah, fine, replied Gabriel. I'm almost done here.

Gina yawned and shook her head. On BBC2, Ethics and Religion had given way to Sport. The supermodels countdown on Channel Five had reached Naomi. Over on Four, Sandra

Bullock was trapped in a rictus smile. On BBC1, credits were running on the reptiles, jaws gaping and snapping on thin air.

Gina drained her whisky and pressed the off button. Whoosh! it went. Amazing how completely the brothel and everything else had vanished. Gina sat for a couple of seconds enjoying the quiet darkness then got to her feet.

Listen, Gabriel, that was a long ten minutes. I'm going up.

Okay, darling, I'll log off.

Gina lay in bed, warm and naked, the way she always slept. Gabriel discarded his clothes and eased himself alongside, putting his arms round her.

Everything okay back home? She mumbled.

I guess so. People are scared though. They say Chavez can't last. Too many people gunning for him. The place is buzzing with rumours of plots. If a coup won't do it, everyone figures the US will try assassination, hire some hit man.

Gina said nothing. It was all so far away. Her life was commonplace, London was commonplace: Gina felt safe with commonplace.

Gabriel snuggled closer.

What were you watching on TV?

Stuff about reptiles, Gina said, with a sudden laugh.

Reptiles? Gabriel said, hoisting himself onto an elbow to peer into Gina's face. I thought you hated reptiles? And it was funny?

Well, it was a mix of reptiles, ethics, and something about men's control over women.

Gabriel considered this briefly as he stretched out again.

Sounds like a weird programme, he said at last. TV in this country is sometimes too serious. It ought to lighten up. Life here is simple, but TV is weird. In Venezuela, TV is simple and life is weird.

Gina was ready to hold Gabriel in her arms. He began to kiss her, up and down her forearms, pressing his lips into the pulse at her wrists, then travelling down to the small of her back. Gently, with both hands, she reached down and pulled his face up to meet hers and kissed him on the nose.

Consolation

MARA TOLD ME she had grown up in a leafy neighbourhood of Oslo. *Leafy*: her command of English idiom was already impeccable, her accent a vanishing trace.

We had come up to Oxford the same day and had met at a reception for philosophy 'freshmen.' Everything about her was original: even her parentage.

She said her Russian father and Spanish mother had been drawn to one another because each reminded the other of the way people were 'back home.' When I shook my head in puzzlement, she threw hers back and laughed. At me, it seemed.

Her mother, she explained, was a leggy blonde from Asturias in flight from Franco, whereas her father was pint-sized and olive-skinned and fleeing from Stalin. I wasn't sure I got the joke.

'They're still together,' she said.

'My parents are from Ipswich,' I said. 'They're like two peas in a pod, and they split up as soon as they thought I was old enough.'

'How old were you?'

'Thirteen.'

'Split peas,' she said.

Norwegian humour, I thought.

Mara was lovely but her loveliness – compounded by the piercing clarity of her thought – petrified me. I felt worse than naked beneath her gaze: I felt transparent.

For two long years, I admired Mara from afar, seeking her

out then avoiding her. Meanwhile I strove to catch up with her reading, to imitate her easy erudition.

She finally noticed me and knocked at my door late one evening, insisting we discuss Kierkegaard, about whom I'd discoursed at length during a seminar that afternoon. In her left hand, she held a copy – in Danish – of *Concluding Unscientific Postscript*; in her right, a bottle of Chianti. 'I don't possess a corkscrew,' she said.

We spent our third year together: by day at classes or in the library; at night in my rooms or her digs. We were inseparable, revising together, practising past exam questions, or debating the scorching philosophical topics of the day: Sartre versus Camus, speech-act theory, Merleau-Ponty's reception of Husserl – that sort of thing. We made love a lot but never spoke the word, taking it somehow for granted.

At Mara's instigation, I took up swimming; at my instigation, she listened to free jazz: we converged effortlessly, spontaneously. And somehow I found an hour a day – usually after she fell asleep – to learn Norwegian, so that when the exams were over we could leave for a holiday in the Fjords. Which we duly did.

That autumn, Mara, with her starred First, moved to the university of Bergen to work on her PhD. Though it was unusual in those days for a man to follow a woman anywhere, I decided to go with her, enrolled in a philosophy MA, and gave English classes. My father said that with my poor Upper Second I should be sensible and sit the civil service exams. My mother sent me a cheque and a note advising me to live a little.

Mara and I found a short-lease, spacious, unfurnished flat behind the bus station. We bought a second-hand bed, cooker, saucepan, some ugly cutlery, and moved in. We would pick up everything else we needed as we went along. It seemed to me we had passed seamlessly into adulthood.

Evenings were our best times. Mara would meet me on the steps of the language school and we would walk round the city, stopping for a coffee or beer if it rained, usually just strolling and talking, keeping an eye open for household furnishings. I should explain that the Scandinavians had not yet discovered the wheely bin: at the end of each day households and businesses simply put their rubbish out on the pavement either in neatly tied bin bags or just as it came. You could find lamp stands, washbasins, bicycles, clothes, cupboards, picture frames, stationery, bedding: for a young couple with a flat to furnish, this seemed a godsend.

So, our eyes raking the pavements for items of utility, we expounded our ideas, conducted our thought experiments, as if hoping to recreate our Oxford idyll. We soon noticed, however, that as our interests in philosophy diverged so our conversations lost their urgency. Mara was now studying the philosophy of mind; I, on the other hand, was exploring Nietzschean aesthetics. As we retreated into the solitude of separate sub-disciplines, the ground we'd shared steadily shrank.

Our peripatetic conversations began to focus on everyday occurrences and situations. Anything could act as springboard: a tramp seen slumped in a doorway might get us riffing on human needs and freedoms; an encounter with some lost, lonely teenager might open onto a discussion of individual responsibility and the social contract; the sight of a bare polystyrene sexless male manikin might trigger a critique of Freud's theories of repression and castration.

Differences in temperament and outlook emerged starkly. I would happily have left these unexamined but for Mara – and I loved her for this – the unexamined life was truly not worth living. We came – for my part, reluctantly – to sense that in important respects we were polar opposites: Mara was a pessimist, I an optimist; she a champion of individual autonomy, while I was more interested in engagement with others.

Sometimes Mara and I debated each another to a speechless and melancholy standstill. Then we would walk in silence, refocusing on the discarded items at the foot of the buildings we passed. Other times, we took refuge in our shared love of word games. One of our favourites was 'collectives.' I'd introduced this to Mara shortly after we'd met. It had come into my family one Christmas after an aged aunt had given my mother a book titled *An Exaltation of Larks*. We had spent the rest of the holiday inventing apposite collectives for people or things. It was the last

Christmas before my father walked out on us. I recall that my mother, a teacher, came up with 'a mendacity of lawyers'; my father, a lawyer, retorted with 'a dither of teachers'; I contributed 'a seething of parents.'

One evening in late October, Mara and I noticed outside a boutique a large black bin bag, its contents betrayed by the jumble of heels, toes, and buckles whose contours showed beneath the filmy plastic. Emptying the bag onto the pavement, we discovered a dozen or so styles of slightly shop-soiled shoes in every adult size. Good footwear is an expensive essential for the Norwegian winter. But as we began avidly to select the styles we preferred and to identify our individual sizes, it dawned on us that all the shoes were for left feet only.

Gazing helplessly at the muddle of smart shoes before us, Mara chuckled and said: "'a disappointment of shoes.'" 'Or "a dejection,"' I suggested.

Other people approached, attracted by the 'disappointment of shoes' and we watched them go through the stages we ourselves had just completed: curiosity, excitement, elation, suspicion, realization, disappointment. Even dejection. Soon there were half a dozen young people, swapping theories or inventing stories to account for the tantalizing find. Had a mass of people lacking right feet visited the shop? Had the machinery of some distant factory, due to a flaw in its construction or calibration, gone berserk, spewing out nothing but left-footed shoes?

A week later, Mara invited three of her new post-grad friends for dinner. By this point we had furnished our flat to our satisfaction. We pointed out our garish curtains, pitted desk, rickety chairs, and mismatched crockery, explaining their provenance, proud of our resourcefulness. One guest – an Austrian – said she'd furnished her studio-flat the same way, then added: 'A curious thing happened last week. After a film at the cinema, we were wandering through the city centre when we happened upon a pile of classy shoes. First we were overjoyed, but we quickly realized they were all for right feet only.' 'Yes, we saw those too,' I said. 'Wait a minute,' Mara interrupted. 'The ones we saw were for *left* feet.' 'No, no,' insisted the Austrian, 'I'm quite sure.' Mara's face fell: 'Which evening was it you went to the cinema?'

We stared at one another as the truth hit home: the boutique had binned over a hundred pairs of serviceable, indeed smart, shoes on successive evenings, as it were, one foot at a time, just to thwart youthful freeloaders like us.

'How could the boutique owner be so mean?' the Austrian asked. 'People who wander the streets checking the refuse are hardly their target clientele,' her companion said. 'It wouldn't even have dented their profits to let a few dozen shoes go for free,' our third guest said.

After they had left, while Mara and I washed the dishes, our minds returned to the 'collectives' word game.

'If that first collection of shoes was a "disappointment,"' I said, the second was "a meanness."'

'Or "a petty-mindedness,"' Mara suggested.

But that was all we could agree on. Whereas I was furious with the boutique, Mara was angry with me and with herself. How could we have failed to work out what was going on? If only we'd realized, we could have taken home the shoes we liked and come back the following day. How could two young philosophers, working in dialectical tandem, suffer such a failure of both the imagination and reason – especially when well motivated because ill shod? Mara's final damning remark was: if two heads were truly better than one, right now those shoes would be on our feet.

I date the disintegration of my relationship with Mara from that evening. She evidently doubted not merely my usefulness as a partner but – and this upset me more, since I experienced it as a philosophical defeat and a personal humiliation – the usefulness of our, indeed of any, partnership; that is to say, she doubted the usefulness of collaborative endeavour itself. On this point I was inconsolable.

We were no longer going out much in the evenings: we'd paid off our debts and were earning at last. Besides, it was too cold now to saunter through the city streets. Mara wrestled with her new field of study while I drowned in Nietzsche's *Nachlass*. We drifted apart.

The following Easter, after a rare meal out to celebrate Mara's birthday, we made love for the first time in weeks. I suppose we didn't know what else to do. I imagined it was for Mara and she probably imagined it was for me. Afterwards, she asked if I was tired. 'Not at all,' I said. 'Let's go into the kitchen and have some wine,' she said.

We sat up late that evening. It was almost like our first days in Oxford, except that by the time the bottle was empty, instead of being back in bed making love, we were still in the kitchen and had agreed to part. Mara's verdict was: 'we just don't add up to anything; we're too dissimilar.' I said I would finish my MA then leave Norway, probably for France. Mara said she'd remain and pursue her studies in Bergen. We'd stay in touch: we'd always be friends.

The following December, after a long gap in our correspondence, I purchased an elegant, Italian pair of fur-lined boots, perfect for Bergen's winter. I packaged them carefully and sent them with a greetings card that read: 'To Mara, in fondest memory: a consolation of shoes.'

On Christmas Day, which I celebrated in Marseilles, I opened a present the contents of which I had guessed from its shape and size: a pair of leather loafers, ideal for the Mediterranean winter. The card read: 'To Tony, with affection: a consolation of shoes.'

No Longer Lonely

I HAD NEVER imagined that dying – my own swiftly approaching death, that is – would be so dispiritingly ordinary, so banal. Nobody knows how to act or what to say, least of all me. Nobody really wants to cry but nobody can quite help it either. It's an embarrassment.

After receiving my lapidary prognosis, I undertook a racketing series of what I now think of as 'lasts.' My last trip into the city centre, which I still love, though all the best shops closed long ago. My last trip to the supermarket, which I had never quite noticed I enjoyed visiting. I said a final goodbye to a cashier, who glanced round as if looking for help. I took leave of the vegetable counter, noticing a new kind of lettuce I had been meaning to try. The following day I took my last walk along our pavement to the postbox. A week ago, I had my last morning downstairs. Yesterday, my final unassisted trip to the lavatory: I fell and couldn't get up so I won't be trying that again. Thus does my little world shrink.

When friends come to see me, I apologize for upsetting their schedule and try to put them at their ease. Their eyes moisten as they squeeze my hand. Some say how strong my grip still feels, as though my hands ought by now to be lying limp upon some lace counterpane. I want to apologize but don't. Family members and relatives are the most awkward. Most of them I haven't seen for years. They tell my husband on the phone how much they want to see me. He never thinks to ask why. They tiptoe into my bedroom, wearing an expression of profound melancholy, take a deep breath, then talk lightheartedly as if their purpose were to cheer me up. I don't have much to say to them. When silence descends, they sniff the air, as if trying to detect the pong of the hereafter. I keep the windows open wider than before. Death really ought to be more frank. It shouldn't creep up the way it does. Couldn't it wear a name badge? Or a t-shirt? Do I seem harsh? Unfeeling? It seems that when dying, you are not supposed to ruffle the sensitivities of those condemned to survive you. Well, to hell with that, I say.

Neighbours drop round and tea is poured for them in my kitchen – which is fine – then I hear them talk in hushed voices to my husband on the stairs and landing. He leads them into the bedroom, softly drawing up chairs by my bed. They peer down on me while they sip. I remain polite. Some talk of their plans: retirement, grandchildren, holidays, that sort of thing. What can I say? 'I do hope you enjoy Goa . . . Derbyshire . . . Brittany. Be sure to send me a postcard! Just in case.'

While I still had my strength, I used my favourite kitchen scissors to shred all my old letters, newspaper cuttings, photos, postcards: these things had meant a great deal to me but they could never mean much to anyone else. Besides, I didn't want to leave a mess for somebody else to clear up. I've always been a tidy person. This process brought back many memories. I emptied the three bottom drawers of my ancient escritoire, filling countless waste-paper baskets. When I finished, I felt somehow cleaner, as if I had emerged from a long hot bath.

Then there were the letters of adieu I received. Some were very touching, but I'm glad they've stopped coming. Few of them required any reply. The best was written by the thirty-something daughter of someone I went to school with. This daughter had had a horrible time as a teenager, had cut off all her hair, even plucked and shaved her eyebrows. One long summer, she came to see me a couple of times every week, told me everything that was happening to her. I'd forgotten all about her but the letter brought it all back. She enclosed a photo of the way she was back then. I suppose you can never tell who will have the best and fondest memories of you. The worst letter was from my son-in-law. Two pages of detail about his flower beds – which I might have enjoyed had I not been grieving over the state of abandonment into which my own garden would now quickly descend – then some forced phrases of appreciation: he praised me for being a 'bullshit detector.' How stilted, I thought. How sad that anyone could deem 'bullshit detection' a rare or special talent of mine. I'm sure I never thought of people or any of their deeds as 'bullshit.' Besides, to my ears 'bullshit' has a brash American ring to it: it's not a term I would ever use.

Quite suddenly everybody stopped coming. The word must have gone out that 'it tires her.' So I'm left to the mercies of the occasional doctor, the twice-daily district nurse, my endlessly tearful husband and three grown-up children, two of whom do so much coming and going that I lose track of their whereabouts: are they downstairs? in Aberdeen? São Paulo? back here again? Even when they are here, they keep going out to the landing to communicate with distant spouses and children, employers and colleagues, clients and creditors, even neighbours who have been tasked to feed their pets. They want to know every medical detail – as if they had suddenly been appointed experts in 'malignancy.' Then they frown and check their watches and mobile phones. When they go, they say with a little air of apology, 'I'm afraid I have to be somewhere else.' Me too, I want to reply.

My other child, my younger son, has cancelled most of his work commitments: 'for the duration,' he said. He has moved down here and installed himself in our little guest room, with his books and computer. His girlfriend joins him at the weekends, which is nice for us all. For the two days she is here, he relaxes, smiles a little more, almost forgets himself. I used never to be sure that his girlfriend was right for him, but I can see it now plain as day. He strives rather frantically to make me comfortable, anticipating my needs, second-guessing even my states of mind; he only leaves my side when I fall asleep. I think he'll be here till the end. I worry about him. He never cries or makes a fuss. I'd like to tell him that I shall die alone even if he is there beside me, holding my hand, but I see no point in upsetting him. I think he imagines that the power of his love can make things less bad. I love him so much but while I croak out the words to tell him so, I have to pull him to me for a long hug, so that he can't see my face. I want him to remember my voice, not my yellow sunken cheeks. He trembles in my arms, then gets up, inhaling desperately, and hurries out of the room. Sweet boy. He doesn't want me to see him cry.

My dreams – and daydreams too – have become more lucid and more shocking and I seem to pass straight into them and come straight out without any warning or transition. The monsters I see recall the ogres that stalked me as a child whenever I had a fever. They emerge from the middle of the wall, straight out of the paper. A few nights ago, I dreamt of a horrid man, tall and thin and leering, dressed in grey clothes and a shiny top hat, who wandered around at my wake, eating all the sandwiches, drinking the sherry, upsetting my mourners. Sometimes I see people I haven't thought of for many decades. About a week ago, I remembered a boy from my primary school, a revolting bully, who attacked me often and brutally. This time I spun round and felled him with a single blow, a sort of karate chop to the neck. I stood over him and watched him breathe his last.

After my younger son's stormy teenage years and our long estrangement, we grew close again listening over and over to Bob Dylan's early albums and somewhat to my surprise many of those songs have been coming back to me. One day I asked my son if he had a copy of *Bringing It All Back Home*, saying that I would like to hear it again with him. He went straight out and bought the CD. I scolded him for being so extravagant. 'It's Alright, Ma,' he replied with an attempt at Dylan's twang. My shallow laughter sparked a coughing fit. When I recovered, I told him that that was precisely the song I wanted to hear: there was a line in it I liked but couldn't quite remember. He selected the song and I took his hand. When we heard Dylan sing, 'For them that think death's honesty won't fall upon them naturally, life sometimes must get lonely,' I squeezed my son's hand hard and he placed his other hand over mine and squeezed back hard.

Now that I've finally stopped eating – it was no longer any pleasure and had become so exhausting – I find I can barely move or talk. Time slips past in endless imaginings and memories: sometimes I cannot tell the difference. My youngest holds my hand and speaks softly. I like silence most now. The nurse comes and goes, asking me kindly to turn this way or that, then thanking me when I do. My husband has retreated to the other side of the bedroom, with my daughter and elder son. This morning I heard the rustle of a newspaper and the clink of a cup.

My mind is fixed on the past now. I dwell again with the first and last person I truly loved without question: my father. How large and bony and cold was his hand, when he held my little hand in his, while we strolled in the city, admiring the shops. Everybody knew him. We couldn't walk five yards. 'Good morning, Mr P. Have you heard about so-and-so? What do you think we should do about such-and-such? And how's your daughter today? Growing very tall, isn't she?' And my father, friendly, solicitous, with a kind word for everyone and a fruit lozenge from a paper bag for every child.

Death is so banal, so dispiriting. But it'll be over in an instant. From life still lived with a mind still capable of passionate thought and feelings – though no one but me knows that now – to sheer nothingness. The difference, the step I have to take, is both too vast and too small. I shall taste life's wonder at the moment it ends. I'm almost ready now. My son holds my hand. If I could just speak again, I'd remind him of the words in that song. I'd just like to tell him that at last, at long last, I'm through with being lonely.

Our Man and the Pigeon

THAT MORNING, AROUND eight, while waiting for a westbound
District-line train, our man noticed at the end of the platform
a huddle of raggedy pigeons competing for dust from a sweets
packet. As the train sped in, slowing with a hiss, a pigeon broke
from its rivals and went to stand alone, craning and bowing
inside the 'G' of MIND THE GAP. The bird moved with a
swinging limp, as if in imitation of a strong-willed old lady suffering with a bad hip. At its throat, from which both down and
feathers had fallen or been ripped, the skin shone pink. The train
stopped, the doors opened. Glancing at the pigeon, our man
boarded the train. Then the pigeon boarded it too.

Our man was heading for work, a decent job in an ugly office
at the other end of the line. He had left his lover warm and
happy in her bed. She could sleep in. She had a day free. She
could do anything or nothing. The whole day long. They hadn't
fallen asleep till late that night. He could remember every word,
every gesture. She might be falling in love with him. He felt he
knew women well enough by this point to recognize the signs
of an incubating love. He would wait for her to phone him.
He wanted to do everything just right this time. This time he
wanted babies.

Our man took a seat next to another man of similar age.
There were several other people in the carriage, some of them
seated behind newspapers. The train clattered on its way. He
glanced toward the doors and saw the pigeon. It was pecking at
the dirt on the floor. He sensed his neighbour had also noticed.

'Just like a hitchhiker,' our man said, chuckling.

'Yeah. He'll probably get out at the next station. They don't travel far,' said the other.

This second man's voice was deep and guttural. He sounded like the kind of man – if there is such a kind – who doesn't care for pigeons. As the train slowed, rocking on its rails, this man got to his expensively shod feet and walked manfully to the door. He carried a heavy folder under one arm. You could tell that no jolt would make him stumble. As if from deference, the pigeon moved to stand against a panel. It seemed to be leaning now. Taking a little weight off its bad hip.

The man-who-probably-didn't-care-for-pigeons got off the train and vanished. He was seen again half way up a flight of stairs marked EXIT, his beige, balding head rising and falling at each step. A press of commuters squeezed onto the train and the doors closed. The pigeon had still not alighted. It continued to lean its scrawny body against the panel, to cock its bullet head this way and that.

At each stop, more passengers got on and as they churned at the doors, our man again sighted the pigeon, appearing now to be clinging to its panel for protection from so many feet. In the aisle, in front of our man, their legs brushing his knees, stood many people, books or screens cradled in their hands, umbrellas hooked to their forearms, some of them hazarding early-morning conversation. Did you watch that programme about such-and-such last night? Have you heard any news of so-and-so . . .?

For a spell our man dozed. It was sudden. He pictured the young man and woman standing in front of him, though apparent strangers, beginning to rub themselves like cats against one another, with not a word spoken, not a glance exchanged. He imagined that he looked round and saw that everybody else was minding their own business. He examined the young people's demeanour, read arousal in both faces. The man was flushed; the woman's eyes flickered, a tongue playing over her front teeth, as for a glamour audition.

Our man awoke to an almost empty carriage. He crossed his legs in reflex modesty, then placed his bag firmly on his lap. The train had surfaced. It was coming to a stop. Soon he would have to stand up. He thought about the day's work ahead of him.

The man-who-probably-didn't-care-for-pigeons had been quite mistaken. The bird was still there, strutting up and down, positively owning the place, seeming to revel in the carriage's near-emptiness.

The train stopped at a station that our man had often used in the past. He hadn't alighted here since separating from his previous girlfriend. He couldn't come through this station without thinking of her, at least momentarily. And now – good heavens! – there she was, standing on the platform opposite, on her way to work, waiting for her eastbound train. He was shocked, scandalized. Could he believe his eyes? But there was no room for doubt.

Our man jumped to his feet to take a better look. Pregnant. She was visibly pregnant. Why?! How?! No – the *how* question was all too elementary and its answer distressing. (Our man felt he still loved her.) But why, *why*? Why with someone else, but not with him? She had sworn she loved him, begged him to stay, conjured him to be patient, striven passionately to explain her reluctance to make babies. She was far too young, she had kept saying. A mere year ago. Yet now . . . As he could see . . . Had she maybe thought he had wanted babies too much? More than he had wanted her? Is it even possible, our man wondered, for a man to want too much to have children?

Two stops later, our man and the pigeon alighted, the latter hopping down on both feet, landing pat. They were above ground, the day had dawned, the sky was grey, the air was fresh. Our man checked his watch, and headed for the exit. Work was summoning him, screaming at him to come in.

Meanwhile the pigeon appeared to take a deep breath, its bare throat filling, as it looked around, high and low, like an old lady performing some healthful neck stretches. Then it fluttered across to the other platform and peered far up the track. Waiting. Waiting.

First Day in Toledo

IT WAS THEIR first full day in Toledo.

Janey had left the hotel quite early to explore the city; Mike had lain in bed, recovering from the gruelling week he'd had at work, back in Luton, shift-work nursing.

This job is fucking killing me, he'd blurted out at two a.m., as they'd stumbled into bed, bloated with cider and tapas.

Stop whingeing! You do exaggerate! Janey had said.

They had agreed to meet in Calle Amirál at eleven. Janey had repeated the name of the street and the time. She had checked Mike had put his watch forward one hour. She had even turned back at the hotel bedroom door and left a note on his bedside table. Mike's time management wasn't fantastic. Janey's was. She took pride in it.

Janey was now standing in Calle Amirál and Mike was five minutes late already.

Typical, she thought. What more could she have done?

Then ten minutes, then fifteen.

Great way to start our holiday, Janey thought, as she ordered a drink in a bar, one eye on the street. This trip was supposed to be good for 'us.' It's starting like shit.

In those days, you may remember, only criminals, cops, and the filthy rich had mobile phones.

Twenty-five minutes, thirty minutes. This was unusual, even for Mike.

If Mike *were* dead, Janey reasoned, there'd be a lot of

practicalities to sort out. In Spanish. Autopsy? *Autopsia*, maybe. Burial? God alone knows. Cremation? *Cremación*? But that might have more to do with creaming than burning. Hell, Mike had never expressed a preference either way. You tend not to, at twenty-eight. His parents of course would take a definite view. They had opinions to burn. Oh, Jesus! Opinions to burn. Not funny.

These are crazy thoughts, she told herself. Of course Mike won't be dead.

She bought a Spanish newspaper, reading what she could. Something was happening in the Basque country, angry protests, a bombing. No surprises there, then.

Forty, forty-five, fifty.

She'd be sad if Mike *were* dead. Gutted. She'd cry, probably. She couldn't remember the last time she'd cried. But she'd cry all right. She loved him. Okay?

Janey found a payphone and rang the hotel. She struggled to explain herself. They eventually put on some guy who spoke English with a Geordie accent but trilling Spanish r's. Janey asked again. Room 49, she said. The Geordie Spaniard said he'd go and look. She would phone back in five minutes. He told her to ask for Manuel. Sure, she said.

Janey walked up and down the street. If Mike didn't come soon, she'd buy some cigarettes. They'd given up together two months ago. If he found her smoking, maybe that would teach him to be late. Oddly, irritatingly, she didn't fancy a cigarette. Yesterday evening, she could have killed for one.

There'd be a simple explanation. Mike would be along soon.

If he *had* done himself in, she'd feel guilty. Recently, he'd been distressed. He'd hated his job ever since he'd been made charge-nurse. He said the government was destroying the NHS. But when weren't they? Then the two of them hadn't been getting on well. Maybe he'd killed himself over her. How would she feel? Was it even possible to kill yourself over someone else? People can do any damn thing, there's no telling. How would he have done it? Hey? What is this? Goddamn Cluedo? With a candlestick or lead piping in the drawing room?

She phoned again. Manuel answered. Mike wasn't in their room. She thanked him. 'Nooooh woR-R-Ries, hen,' he said. Janey burst out laughing.

If Mike were dead somewhere, she'd be alone. And not just to pick up the pieces. After too. But she'd been alone before. It had its advantages. She looked around, watched people strolling by. She noticed a lad serving at the bar – a young man, actually, not a 'lad' at all – admired the turn of his legs when he took drinks out to a table. Good skin. The young man noticed her noticing him. He smiled, flicked some hair out of his eyes. She smiled right back. Well, as one door closes, another opens.

Besides, it was too soon to panic. She would wait a little longer then go to the police. They would contact the hospitals for her. Maybe he'd been run over. Just hurt. That can happen. He could have stepped out in front of a bus, looking the wrong way. A simple mistake.

She walked round the block but returned to the same bar. The cute barman pretended not to see her sit down. She wasn't going to look up and down the street for Mike any more. He could bloody well find her.

From her pocket she pulled out a novel by Ali Smith. She read it for a couple of minutes then put it face down on the table. She gazed into space. Why don't writers write about characters you could actually care about?

While that thought decayed, Mike, her boyfriend, fiancé, latest squeeze, the future father of her still unimagined children, the man who would one day leave her for an older woman – an *older* woman: the final insult – tapped her lightly on the shoulder.

I thought you were dead, she said. Where the hell were you?

He gestured at the novel. Upset were you?

She shrugged. So what happened?

Nothing. I overslept.

What, till twelve thirty?

It's only twelve twenty now, he said, pointing at his watch. It was half-eleven when I woke.

And it took you fifty minutes to get your ass over here?

I needed a shower. Should I have come in my pyjamas?

You weren't wearing any.

Anyway, I walked ten minutes in the wrong direction.

Dickhead.

I'm parched, Mike said. Are you going to get me that drink?

Janey heaved a deep sigh, dragged herself up and went to the bar. For a moment I really thought he was fucking dead, she murmured, looking into the barman's dreamy eyes.

The Simplest Thing

LIVIA? *ECCOMI* . . .

So now I'm here. Remember me? It's Gerhard – as if you wouldn't recognize my voice. We were together for eight years, for heaven's sake. Almost nine. We were lovers – *amanti, liebhaber.* How obsolete those words now sound . . .

Your sister has gone to get something to eat and your parents have left for the night. They looked shattered. They've sat with you all day. They said they'll be back tomorrow. They acted astonished when they saw me, though surely your sister must have mentioned I was coming. They never liked me. Quite apart from the German 'question'. Even after you took me to Marzabotto. What was I supposed to do?

Last night, after your sister phoned, I started wondering what to say to you. On the plane down from Frankfurt this afternoon, I sat thinking up lines like it was for a first date. I hadn't had to think about whether or not to come. My kids hardly notice me when I'm there, so why would they miss me while I'm gone? As for my wife and my job . . . I'll come to that. Unless you regain consciousness first.

It's been nineteen years since we split up. Okay, since I walked out. Frankly, Livia, you're not looking great. Giovanna warned me you were badly banged up, your face especially. What shocks me is how pale your skin is. You always used to be so healthily tanned yet somehow rosy-cheeked. Maybe it's the drugs they're giving you. Still, I can see from that arm and the general lie of the blankets that you're not particularly overweight. I always imagined you would run to fat. So, well done for that! As for the accident: what the hell were you thinking? Riding pillion on a motorbike? Without a helmet? Giovanna said your car had run out of petrol on account of a faulty fuel gauge. It was a quiet country road above Sassuolo, lunchtime, zero traffic. It was probably raining, she said. All the same, couldn't you have waited for a car? You must need your head examining. Christ! Sorry about that . . . Still, you know what I mean.

I hope you've forgiven me for walking out on you all those years ago. I had never hit a woman before and I was so glad when you hit me back. I know you didn't want me to go. The day before, when I saw you coming at me with that carving knife, I had a moment of stark illumination about the state of our relationship: I just skipped any notion of mending things and went straight to 'Run!' Perhaps that was cowardly of me. A couple of years later, when you wrote to my parents asking for my address, I was delighted. I hadn't expected ever to hear from you. And it's been so good to receive your news occasionally.

Yet don't you think it's a little odd that Giovanna thought of calling me – of all people? She said you sometimes mention me and never show any trace of bitterness. To be precise, she actually said 'mentioned,' using the imperfect – '*accennava*.' I still notice things like that.

At the airport, the second thing I said to Giovanna was, 'How do you talk to someone in a coma whom you jilted years ago? . . .' 'What matters is that you're here now,' she said. 'Just act natural.'

Natural. Right. Well, I can try that.

If you come round suddenly, just how surprised will you be to find me sitting here? You're bound to recognize me: I've not changed much. By the time we split up, I'd already lost most of my hair. What was left quickly went grey back in Germany. I suppose I've put on some more weight. Too much sausage and sauerkraut and beer: eight years in Italy never made a dent on my eating habits. These days I wear loose-fitting shirts. Still, I'm hoping to stay out of elasticated trousers a while longer.

As you'll have remembered by now, I'm not much of a talker. If you fall asleep the moment you hear my voice, I'll not blame you. If you're 'locked in,' please don't worry about letting your mind wander. I wouldn't take offence even if I could tell. The nurse said I should be 'positive' and pretend you're listening and imagine that I need to make an effort to hold your attention. I'm trying to simulate that right now. I'm just not a good talker. I repeat myself, don't I? For some reason, I tend to say things twice. A shrink once told me I lacked confidence: I don't expect people to pay any attention to what I say. So I say it again. Cost me the earth, that shrink.

Flying always takes it out of me. That's the only reason I'm yawning. Tomorrow I'll tell you about my wife. Then my kids. Then work. After that, if I feel you've not suffered enough, I'll discuss regional politics in Rhine-Westphalia. That ought to bring you steaming out of your coma like Glenn Close from the bathtub, railing against the abuse of the comatose. Well – given the opportunity – who could fail to abuse the comatose? One can't say kind, cuddly things for ever. The comatose must surely be one of the most brow-beaten groups in society. Subjected round the clock to the loving attention of their self-appointing nearest and dearest – with no hope of retaliation. After all, if you do manage to jolt someone back into the here and now, they're not likely to sue you for abuse.

The nurse said your eyes flicker sometimes, so I'm watching closely. She said they open just a crack, like a cat-flap blown in briefly by a gust of wind. Fancy a nurse coming up with an image like that. 'You must have cats,' I said to her. She pulled a face, as if she thought I might be flirting. 'I hate cats,' she said. 'I'm allergic. I keep hamsters. Hamsters don't moult. But everybody knows about cat-flaps.' Then she turned her back on me. Nurses can be so impolite. I can't blame her, though. Just try imagining that woman's life: all day on the coma ward, then home to the hamsters. There's no way she has a husband or partner, is there? What grown man – or woman – would want to share a house with hamsters?

Anyway, Giovanna said the doctors think you may regain consciousness any time. 'Miracles are commoner than people think,' they told her.

I'm beginning to notice how odd this is, this talking-to-the-comatose thing. You don't know what to assume and yet you have to be careful what you say – in case they ever come round. Nevertheless, I feel this isn't the moment to indulge in half-truths, mince one's words or take refuge in euphemism.

So I'll talk. I've got all night. And so the hell have you – no offence intended! I'll stay at least till Giovanna gets back, then I expect I'll have a coffee and hang around a while longer. I'll hear her news, bore her stiff with mine. We'll stand outside the glass door and talk about you. Maybe in hushed voices. I'll catch up on sleep tomorrow, while your family's all over you. I'm in no hurry to go anywhere. Nobody's waiting for me back in Germany. I'm between jobs. And my wife's having an affair. You probably don't want to know about that. It bores even me. I'll tell you about it later.

It's odd, sitting up with you late at night. It's almost like old times. We were always nocturnal, weren't we? That would be the wrong place to start. Natural enough, but wrong.

I might give you my version of how you and I broke up. Perhaps you think I have already. That snippet was my unique perspective on the carving-knife moment. I'm not blaming you. A lot of people would give their eye teeth to have their ex – let alone their spouse, partner, latest squeeze – stretched out inca-pacitated long enough to have to listen. But I'm not going to exploit my advantage to press a point. My wife, for example, is always screaming, 'You never LISTEN!' What she can't under-stand is that, even without listening, I hear far too much.

I'm going to talk more or less continuously. I'll see if I can jog your memory a bit. Assuming you're there. Try flickering an eye – like a cat-flap or not. I can wait you out. Go on. For me. Nothing doing? Maybe later.

I'll tell you everything. I won't hold back. All the things I never told you when we were together. Just as they pop into my mind. I'll try to annoy you into waking up. I'd really like to see that lopsided smile I used to love so much – that I would still love, if it can still exist – I told you I'm not a good talker. I'm sorry to see you in this state, you know. I probably should have said that first – got it off my chest.

Over the next few days, I'm going to give you my version of our love affair. You've never heard it. I'm going to confess to things I always denied. Well, to one thing actually. Cristina. You were always accusing me of fancying her and I never did. In the end she stopped coming round. You were the most jealous person I've ever met. Or *are*. (I must watch my tenses.)

And you were so prickly, so terrified of criticism, but eager to dish it out. Sitting here close beside you, the years drop away. All those 'issues' we used to have: I'm beginning to remember them now, without you even being conscious. Now you're nailed to this bed, all your loved ones are going to tell you exactly what they always thought of you, once the lovey-dovey stuff has been got through. I could really give you some home truths. You had certain habits I found downright unsanitary. Shall I go on about them? Who's to stop me? You never hear of anyone emerging from a coma, saying, 'it's just not true what you said about me . . .! How dare you!'

I'll start by recalling how we met and those first few days. It was all so beautiful. Truly, Livia, I don't think you ever realized that you swept me off my feet. Women aren't supposed to do that, are they? Men are expected to do all the sweeping. I was dazed . . .

My memories of those first hours and weeks are so sharp in my mind. If I let my focus soften a little on your face, the swelling and bruising quickly fall away and your hair returns to its original colour and thickness, and your lines slowly fade. Though, to be blunt, it's easier if I shut my eyes.

I first met you at the home of an acquaintance who had helped me move in. Ottavio was his name and he owned a van. You were friends with his girlfriend, Daniela. Remember? You'd bounced into that huge apartment they shared in Via San Felice, driving a ripple of merriment before you. I didn't think you'd noticed me. Anyway, either Ottavio or Daniela must have told you where I lived. So two days later, there you stood at my door, asking me out, fidgeting, chewing at a wet clump of hair that was wagging at the corner of your mouth.

That evening we went out. Walked all round the city, with you playing guide. It was freezing, early February. I had no idea it could be that cold in Italy. You led me down Via del Pratello. I had my very first bowl of piping hot *pasta e fagioli*. (Beans with pasta have held a curiously erotic charge for me ever since.) Then, walking back towards the university area, you suddenly stopped chattering and backed into a doorway, up a step, caught my hand, and faced me. I must have looked stupid, staring at you in astonishment. You grabbed me by a lapel and pulled me towards you. The way you made love to me that night made love seem the simplest thing. Two days later, you moved your belongings – one small suitcase, one large hold-all – into my flat. It took me a few weeks to catch up, but catch up I did.

Then you started getting paranoid, hallucinating all kinds of liaisons that I simply never had, never wanted. Even when I managed to convince you I wasn't having it away with your latest suspect, I could never convince you that I didn't want to. We stopped seeing almost all your female friends, even those happily paired off, even Gina and Roberta, lesbians for christsakes. You might have thought they'd be safe. But back then, I suppose, everybody was sleeping with everybody else. Whereas I didn't have an unfaithful bone in my body. Call it love . . .

I wish you'd wake up, hit me, even brandish that knife again. You're the only woman I ever hit, did I tell you that? It's a distinction of a sort. I always knew you'd hit me back harder. That was so reassuring. I'm repeating myself. Again.

Looking at you now, recalling the way you were, I see I've led a dull life since we broke up. My parents of course were relieved and happy when I returned home. They had longed to see me settled. When I resumed and finished my law degree, they were beside themselves. They went to their graves perfectly contented. What price can you put on that? To be happy and proud for all eternity . . . And I haven't been unhappy myself. At least not deeply. I specialized in labour law and did a lot of pro bono work, fighting greedy capitalist exploiters one case at a time. Small stuff, but satisfying.

One question – by far the most important one – which I've wanted to ask you all these years is: do you ever think back to the sex we had? Maybe women just don't reminisce about sex. Men do, I can tell you. At least I do. I've never had sex like that again. But then perhaps you have. Maybe a lot better. I appreciate your silence on this matter. That was a joke, okay? But not a good one? No. Recently, I've given up on sex altogether. With my wife, at any rate. There probably aren't many men who'd admit that. One day she told me she didn't enjoy it any more. Just like that. Well, fine, I said. Fine. Of course I was absolutely wretched, but I was damned if I was going to show it. It felt like the last straw and I now see that it was. I'd rather jerk off on my own in a toilet than make love to someone who's suppressing a yawn. So there it is. And now she's having an affair. I don't blame her. Not a bit. I just wish I could kill her. We pretend we don't mind. We hope it'll blow over. We – modern men. We'd slit their throats, if we could get away with it. I've read all the self-help books. They tell you it's all about understanding and being tolerant and giving one's partner space and that relationships can be saved and even strengthened by a little dalliance. *Cazzate!*

Do you remember how I wept at Marzabotto? You found it shocking. In fact, that was just about the only time in my adult life I've wept. It's not that I'm strong or especially insensitive. I'm just not a weeper. I didn't even cry when my parents died. At Marzabotto, I don't think I was weeping for the massacred dead. I wept for myself. The scale of that history made me feel completely insignificant and indelibly guilty. Nazi crimes were all my fault. Well before I was born. And I was going to have to live and die with that knowledge. The next day, your great-aunt showed me the place behind the barn where *partigiani* had come to pick up messages and had sometimes hidden out for a night. She talked to me really nicely with her voice but her lips remained stiff and hard like a rope ringing her smile. I couldn't stop talking and grinning, trying so hard to be inoffensive, a good German, goddamnit. In the end you whispered to me: Calm down! She hasn't talked to a German in over forty years and the last one was wearing uniform and had a gun. She's making a huge effort.

The other thing that's been weighing on me has to do with Cristina. You know – or ought to know – that she was never my type. Dishy in a way I never found interesting. I can't explain. I never went for the voluptuous type. I'm sure she never fancied me either. Still, you had driven her away with your jealousy. I'd just like to tell you that we actually did 'hook up' as they say, one time. God I hate the way kids speak nowadays. 'Hooked up': how can it be possible to be so euphemistic and so vulgar at one and the same time? But here's what happened. I bumped into her one day in that anarchist bookshop, *Il Picchio* – two doors down from our flat. Does that place still exist? You were at work. I hadn't seen Cristina for months. We chatted a little, embarrassed, then all of a sudden she invited me to her place for a cup of tea. I didn't know how to say 'no.' We talked about you. Laughed about your insane paranoia. Declared we'd never been remotely attracted to each other . . . I don't know how it happened. I don't think either of us took a decision as such, but as soon as we'd cleared the air – so to speak – we were all over each other. It was like we deserved it. To be exact, it was like we had earned it. Paid for it. Paid in advance and in full. It was nothing special. We agreed on that. We weren't tempted to repeat the experiment. It was just a free fuck – free in every way. Outside of history. Do you know what I mean? No? So get up and slap me . . .

I can see your sister through the glass. I guess she found something to eat somewhere. She's having a coffee from the machine. She can see I'm still talking. She's waiting till I finish. She's sipping her coffee from a tiny cardboard cup. It's two shades of brown on the outside and has two little flaps sticking out forming a tiny handle. Machine coffee. I'll have one soon. I'll say goodbye to you for now and tell Giovanna I think I saw a flicker, a tiny flicker. It's a lie, but where's the harm? I'll tell her I'll be back late tomorrow afternoon. Then I'll leave. I'll go to my hotel and sleep, maybe read a paper first to relax me. I'll wake around noon, have something to eat, walk around the town a little. Just to see what I can remember. I'll go to some of the places we used to go. I'll see if that bookshop, Il Picchio, still exists. I'll tell you about my day tomorrow evening. Before I go, there's something else I wanted to say. Don't worry, it isn't about you. I've had this thought in the back of mind ever since I got here. It's a memory.

I once observed this family group, a large extended family, sitting outside at a restaurant, eating an evening meal. I think they were Danes or Swedes. There was a screaming toddler, who kept being passed from mother to father and back again. It was hopeless. Then this grand-dad or great-uncle or whoever the hell he was decided to take charge of the situation. He got the kid's dad to put the kid in the buggy and then he marched off with the kid strapped down and howling. The pair of them could be seen for about twenty minutes, appearing and disappearing in different parts of the square, coming out of side streets, turning corners. Eventually, just as I was paying the bill, the old man arrived back at his family's table, beaming triumphantly, like he'd just scaled Mount Everest. The toddler was red-faced, snotty-nosed, but asleep at last. The old man had worn the kid out.' People looked at him admiringly and he said something like, 'You just have to show them who's boss.'

Idiotic? Of course. Totally. Yet, right now, it's exactly how I feel with you. I feel like that old uncle or grandad must have felt: I'm going to wait you out. I'm not having you beat me. You hear? I can be more stubborn than any damn person idiotic enough – even momentarily – to ride pillion without a helmet. In the rain! Probably . . . The thing is – and I worked this out during the flight – I didn't have any plans to see you again ever. But now I think about it, I know you were the greatest love I ever had. And if this thing hadn't happened, maybe I'd have got in touch with you again some day. Maybe when we were in our seventies. Or eighties. That happens, doesn't it? We might have become friends again in our declining years – who knows? – maybe even lovers. It wasn't over, was it? Wake up and tell me I'm wrong . . .

Surly Child

BENNY WAS A dull-looking boy. He walked several paces behind his parents each day to school. When the headteacher told him to stand up he stared straight ahead until told again, and only then stood up – and slowly. An insolent, intractable, surly child, everyone thought. When his mother, an ashen blonde in tweeds and cashmeres fetched him from the playground at home time, neither adult nor child said a word in greeting, neither cracked a smile.

Jim, with whom Benny shared a desk, tried to make friends. Benny turned away. Jim noticed that Benny liked insects. Benny smiled when Jim showed him a photograph of a tarantula. Jim said he had a house full of spiders and could bring Benny one. Benny imagined a tarantula and said, Okay. Jim brought Benny a large harmless hirsute spider in a matchbox and showed it to Benny at break time. Jim was the first person for many months to see Benny laugh.

But Benny imagined his parents' reaction and told Jim he couldn't keep the spider. Jim watched Benny's lower lip tremble and expected him to cry but then he didn't.

Every day Jim brought the spider to school and every day Benny let it walk on his skin and scuttle over his clothes. The other children looked on in silence. The teachers observed from a distance. Benny had a friend.

Christopher Woodall grew up on the outer reaches of London. After time adrift with student friends in Northern Germany, Scandinavia, Southern Europe, and East Africa, he was part-educated at the universities of Cambridge and Bordeaux, before remaining for almost a decade in Italy, where he worked as a language teacher and translator. Woodall's formative experience came in 1976 when, with little French and less direction, he joined a band of mostly migrant workers on the nightshift of a metals and plastics factory in Southeast France. This year-long encounter eventually provided the starting point for November, Woodall's debut novel, published by Dalkey in 2016. Writing in the journal Race and Class, Chris Searle has described November as "startling and deeply empathetic." Currently engaged in a number of writing projects, including a sequel to *November*, Woodall also continues to translate. His published translations include Lydie Salvayre's *The Company of Ghosts* (Dalkey Archive, 2006) and Massimo Carlotto's *The Colombian Mule* (Europa, 2013). Christopher lives in Europe with his partner and their son.

MICHAL AJVAZ, *The Golden Age.*
The Other City.

PIERRE ALBERT-BIROT, *Grabinoulor.*

YUZ ALESHKOVSKY, *Kangaroo.*

FELIPE ALFAU, *Chromos.*
Locos.

JOE AMATO, *Samuel Taylor's Last Night.*

IVAN ÂNGELO, *The Celebration.*
The Tower of Glass.

ANTÓNIO LOBO ANTUNES, *Knowledge of Hell.*
The Splendor of Portugal.

ALAIN ARIAS-MISSON, *Theatre of Incest.*

JOHN ASHBERY & JAMES SCHUYLER,
A Nest of Ninnies.

ROBERT ASHLEY, *Perfect Lives.*

GABRIELA AVIGUR-ROTEM, *Heatwave and Crazy Birds.*

DJUNA BARNES, *Ladies Almanack.*
Ryder.

JOHN BARTH, *Letters.*
Sabbatical.

DONALD BARTHELME, *The King.*
Paradise.

SVETISLAV BASARA, *Chinese Letter.*

MIQUEL BAUÇÀ, *The Siege in the Room.*

RENÉ BELLETTO, *Dying.*

MAREK BIENCZYK, *Transparency.*

ANDREI BITOV, *Pushkin House.*

ANDREJ BLATNIK, *You Do Understand.*
Law of Desire.

LOUIS PAUL BOON, *Chapel Road.*
My Little War.
Summer in Termuren.

ROGER BOYLAN, *Killoyle.*

IGNÁCIO DE LOYOLA BRANDÃO,
Anonymous Celebrity.
Zero.

BONNIE BREMSER, *Troia: Mexican Memoirs.*

CHRISTINE BROOKE-ROSE,
Amalgamemnon.

BRIGID BROPHY, *In Transit.*
The Prancing Novelist.

GERALD L. BRUNS,
Modern Poetry and the Idea of Language.

GABRIELLE BURTON, *Heartbreak Hotel.*

MICHEL BUTOR, *Degrees.*
Mobile.

G. CABRERA INFANTE, *Infante's Inferno.*
Three Trapped Tigers.

JULIETA CAMPOS, *The Fear of Losing Eurydice.*

ANNE CARSON, *Eros the Bittersweet.*

ORLY CASTEL-BLOOM, *Dolly City.*

LOUIS-FERDINAND CÉLINE, *North.*
Conversations with Professor Y.
London Bridge.

MARIE CHAIX, *The Laurels of Lake Constance.*

HUGO CHARTERIS, *The Tide Is Right.*

ERIC CHEVILLARD, *Demolishing Nisard.*
The Author and Me.

MARC CHOLODENKO, *Mordechai Schamz.*

JOSHUA COHEN, *Witz.*

EMILY HOLMES COLEMAN, *The Shutter of Snow.*

ERIC CHEVILLARD, *The Author and Me.*

ROBERT COOVER, *A Night at the Movies.*

STANLEY CRAWFORD, *Log of the S.S. The Mrs Unguentine.*
Some Instructions to My Wife.

RENÉ CREVEL, *Putting My Foot in It.*

RALPH CUSACK, *Cadenza.*

NICHOLAS DELBANCO, *Sherbrookes.*
The Count of Concord.

NIGEL DENNIS, *Cards of Identity.*

PETER DIMOCK, *A Short Rhetoric for Leaving the Family.*

ARIEL DORFMAN, *Konfidenz.*

COLEMAN DOWELL, *Island People.*
Too Much Flesh and Jabez.

ARKADII DRAGOMOSHCHENKO,
Dust.

RIKKI DUCORNET, *Phosphor in Dreamland.*
The Complete Butcher's Tales.

FOR A FULL LIST OF PUBLICATIONS, VISIT: www.dalkeyarchive.com

JACQUES JOUET, *Mountain R.*
Savage.
Upstaged.
MIEKO KANAI, *The Word Book.*
YORAM KANIUK, *Life on Sandpaper.*
ZURAB KARUMIDZE, *Dagny.*
JOHN KELLY, *From Out of the City.*
HUGH KENNER, *Flaubert, Joyce
and Beckett: The Stoic Comedians.*
Joyce's Voices.
DANILO KIŠ, *The Attic.*
The Lute and the Scars.
Psalm 44.
A Tomb for Boris Davidovich.
ANITA KONKKA, *A Fool's Paradise.*
GEORGE KONRÁD, *The City Builder.*
TADEUSZ KONWICKI, *A Minor
Apocalypse.*
The Polish Complex.
ANNA KORDZAIA-SAMADASHVILI,
Me, Margarita.
MENIS KOUMANDAREAS, *Koula.*
ELAINE KRAF, *The Princess of 72nd Street.*
JIM KRUSOE, *Iceland.*
AYSE KULIN, *Farewell: A Mansion in
Occupied Istanbul.*
EMILIO LASCANO TEGUI, *On Elegance
While Sleeping.*
ERIC LAURRENT, *Do Not Touch.*
VIOLETTE LEDUC, *La Bâtarde.*
EDOUARD LEVÉ, *Autoportrait.*
Newspaper.
Suicide.
Works.
MARIO LEVI, *Istanbul Was a Fairy Tale.*
DEBORAH LEVY, *Billy and Girl.*
JOSÉ LEZAMA LIMA, *Paradiso.*
ROSA LIKSOM, *Dark Paradise.*
OSMAN LINS, *Avalovara.*
The Queen of the Prisons of Greece.
FLORIAN LIPUŠ, *The Errors of Young Tjaž.*
GORDON LISH, *Peru.*
ALF MACLOCHLAINN, *Out of Focus.*
Past Habitual.

The Corpus in the Library.
RON LOEWINSOHN, *Magnetic Field(s).*
YURI LOTMAN, *Non-Memoirs.*
D. KEITH MANO, *Take Five.*
MINA LOY, *Stories and Essays of Mina Loy.*
MICHELINE AHARONIAN MARCOM,
A Brief History of Yes.
The Mirror in the Well.
BEN MARCUS, *The Age of Wire and String.*
WALLACE MARKFIELD, *Teitlebaum's
Window.*
DAVID MARKSON, *Reader's Block.*
Wittgenstein's Mistress.
CAROLE MASO, *AVA.*
HISAKI MATSUURA, *Triangle.*
LADISLAV MATEJKA & KRYSTYNA
POMORSKA, EDS., *Readings in Russian
Poetics: Formalist & Structuralist Views.*
HARRY MATHEWS, *Cigarettes.*
The Conversions.
The Human Country.
The Journalist.
My Life in CIA.
Singular Pleasures.
The Sinking of the Odradek.
Stadium.
Tlooth.
HISAKI MATSUURA, *Triangle.*
DONAL MCLAUGHLIN, *beheading the
virgin mary, and other stories.*
JOSEPH MCELROY, *Night Soul and
Other Stories.*
ABDELWAHAB MEDDEB, *Talismano.*
GERHARD MEIER, *Isle of the Dead.*
HERMAN MELVILLE, *The Confidence-
Man.*
AMANDA MICHALOPOULOU, *I'd Like.*
STEVEN MILLHAUSER, *The Barnum
Museum.*
In the Penny Arcade.
RALPH J. MILLS, JR., *Essays on Poetry.*
MOMUS, *The Book of Jokes.*
CHRISTINE MONTALBETTI, *The Origin
of Man.*
Western.

NICHOLAS MOSLEY, *Accident.*
Assassins.
Catastrophe Practice.
A Garden of Trees.
Hopeful Monsters.
Imago Bird.
Inventing God.
Look at the Dark.
Metamorphosis.
Natalie Natalia.
Serpent.
WARREN MOTTE, *Fables of the Novel:*
French Fiction since 1990.
Fiction Now: The French Novel in the
21st Century.
Mirror Gazing.
Oulipo: A Primer of Potential Literature.
GERALD MURNANE, *Barley Patch.*
Inland.
YVES NAVARRE, *Our Share of Time.*
Sweet Tooth.
DOROTHY NELSON, *In Night's City.*
Tar and Feathers.
ESHKOL NEVO, *Homesick.*
WILFRIDO D. NOLLEDO, *But for*
the Lovers.
BORIS A. NOVAK, *The Master of*
Insomnia.
FLANN O'BRIEN, *At Swim-Two-Birds.*
The Best of Myles.
The Dalkey Archive.
The Hard Life.
The Poor Mouth.
The Third Policeman.
CLAUDE OLLIER, *The Mise-en-Scène.*
Wert and the Life Without End.
PATRIK OUŘEDNÍK, *Europeana.*
The Opportune Moment, 1855.
BORIS PAHOR, *Necropolis.*
FERNANDO DEL PASO, *News from*
the Empire.
Palinuro of Mexico.
ROBERT PINGET, *The Inquisitory.*
Mahu or The Material.
Trio.
MANUEL PUIG, *Betrayed by Rita*
Hayworth.

The Buenos Aires Affair.
Heartbreak Tango.
RAYMOND QUENEAU, *The Last Days.*
Odile.
Pierrot Mon Ami.
Saint Glinglin.
ANN QUIN, *Berg.*
Passages.
Three.
Tripticks.
ISHMAEL REED, *The Free-Lance*
Pallbearers.
The Last Days of Louisiana Red.
Ishmael Reed: The Plays.
Juice!
The Terrible Threes.
The Terrible Twos.
Yellow Back Radio Broke-Down.
JASIA REICHARDT, *15 Journeys Warsaw*
to London.
JOÃO UBALDO RIBEIRO, *House of the*
Fortunate Buddhas.
JEAN RICARDOU, *Place Names.*
RAINER MARIA RILKE,
The Notebooks of Malte Laurids Brigge.
JULIÁN RÍOS, *The House of Ulysses.*
Larva: A Midsummer Night's Babel.
Poundemonium.
ALAIN ROBBE-GRILLET, *Project for a*
Revolution in New York.
A Sentimental Novel.
AUGUSTO ROA BASTOS, *I the Supreme.*
DANIËL ROBBERECHTS, *Arriving in*
Avignon.
JEAN ROLIN, *The Explosion of the*
Radiator Hose.
OLIVIER ROLIN, *Hotel Crystal.*
ALIX CLEO ROUBAUD, *Alix's Journal.*
JACQUES ROUBAUD, *The Form of*
a City Changes Faster, Alas, Than the
Human Heart.
The Great Fire of London.
Hortense in Exile.
Hortense Is Abducted.
Mathematics: The Plurality of Worlds of
Lewis.
Some Thing Black.

FOR A FULL LIST OF PUBLICATIONS, VISIT: www.dalkeyarchive.com

RAYMOND ROUSSEL, *Impressions of Africa.*

VEDRANA RUDAN, *Night.*

PABLO M. RUIZ, *Four Cold Chapters on the Possibility of Literature.*

GERMAN SADULAEV, *The Maya Pill.*

TOMAŽ ŠALAMUN, *Soy Realidad.*

LYDIE SALVAYRE, *The Company of Ghosts.*
The Lecture.
The Power of Flies.

LUIS RAFAEL SÁNCHEZ, *Macho Camacho's Beat.*

SEVERO SARDUY, *Cobra & Maitreya.*

NATHALIE SARRAUTE, *Do You Hear Them?*
Martereau.
The Planetarium.

STIG SÆTERBAKKEN, *Siamese.*
Self-Control.
Through the Night.

ARNO SCHMIDT, *Collected Novellas.*
Collected Stories.
Nobodaddy's Children.
Two Novels.

ASAF SCHURR, *Motti.*

GAIL SCOTT, *My Paris.*

DAMION SEARLS, *What We Were Doing and Where We Were Going.*

JUNE AKERS SEESE,
Is This What Other Women Feel Too?

BERNARD SHARE, *Inish.*
Transit.

VIKTOR SHKLOVSKY, *Bowstring.*
Literature and Cinematography.
Theory of Prose.
Third Factory.
Zoo, or Letters Not about Love.

PIERRE SINIAC, *The Collaborators.*

KJERSTI A. SKOMSVOLD,
The Faster I Walk, the Smaller I Am.

JOSEF ŠKVORECKÝ, *The Engineer of Human Souls.*

GILBERT SORRENTINO, *Aberration of Starlight.*
Blue Pastoral.
Crystal Vision.

Imaginative Qualities of Actual Things.
Mulligan Stew. Red the Fiend.
Steelwork.
Under the Shadow.

MARKO SOSIČ, *Ballerina, Ballerina.*

ANDRZEJ STASIUK, *Dukla.*
Fado.

GERTRUDE STEIN, *The Making of Americans.*
A Novel of Thank You.

LARS SVENDSEN, *A Philosophy of Evil.*

PIOTR SZEWC, *Annihilation.*

GONÇALO M. TAVARES, *A Man: Klaus Klump.*
Jerusalem.
Learning to Pray in the Age of Technique.

LUCIAN DAN TEODOROVICI,
Our Circus Presents...

NIKANOR TERATOLOGEN, *Assisted Living.*

STEFAN THEMERSON, *Hobson's Island.*
The Mystery of the Sardine.
Tom Harris.

TAEKO TOMIOKA, *Building Waves.*

JOHN TOOMEY, *Sleepwalker.*

DUMITRU TSEPENEAG, *Hotel Europa.*
The Necessary Marriage.
Pigeon Post.
Vain Art of the Fugue.

ESTHER TUSQUETS, *Stranded.*

DUBRAVKA UGRESIC, *Lend Me Your Character.*
Thank You for Not Reading.

TOR ULVEN, *Replacement.*

MATI UNT, *Brecht at Night.*
Diary of a Blood Donor.
Things in the Night.

ÁLVARO URIBE & OLIVIA SEARS, EDS.,
Best of Contemporary Mexican Fiction.

ELOY URROZ, *Friction.*
The Obstacles.

LUISA VALENZUELA, *Dark Desires and the Others.*
He Who Searches.

PAUL VERHAEGHEN, *Omega Minor.*

BORIS VIAN, *Heartsnatcher.*

FOR A FULL LIST OF PUBLICATIONS, VISIT: www.dalkeyarchive.com

CPSIA information can be obtained
at www.ICGtesting.com
Printed in the USA
BVHW070922301218
536649BV00006B/8/P

9 781628 972924